Long Trail Home

Wagon Train Matches

Lacy Williams

Chapter One

"Either you get married or leave the wagon train." The words seemed to echo in the sudden silence between the group of travelers.

Coop Spencer had been at odds with his Maker since birth, but for once in his sorry life he was filled with such a profound sense of relief and happiness that he very nearly sent a prayer of thanks heavenward.

Hollis Tremblay, the wagonmaster of the Oregon-bound company Coop was traveling with, stared expectantly at Coop and the young woman standing beside him. Belle.

Coop realized for one wild moment that he didn't know her last name.

But Hollis's demand was about to give Coop a chance at happiness he hadn't dared to imagine for himself.

The other two folks completed the circle—Jason Goodwin, the company's doctor, and his new wife, Maddie. Friends of Hollis and of Belle, too... of a sort. They seemed to be holding their combined breath as they waited on someone—Coop or Belle—to answer Hollis's demand.

"I'll do it." Coop was proud of the way he kept his voice even. When he finally looked down at the woman beside him, his voice softened even more. "I'll marry you."

But instead of a smile or a word of thanks that he'd stepped in to make things right for her, her eyes flashed. She spun on her heel and marched away.

Coop's pulse slammed in his temples and the potential happiness fizzing in his stomach turned sour.

He started after her, but not before Maddie caught Belle's elbow and fell into step with her.

"I've got things to attend to," Hollis called out from where they'd left him.

"Belle—" Maddie started.

"I won't do it," the younger woman muttered. Even from a few strides behind her, Coop saw the flare of color high in her cheeks when her head turned.

"Hold up a minute," Doc said. Coop hadn't realized the other man was just behind him until Doc caught Coop's arm in one hand.

Coop whirled on him, threw off the hold.

Doc didn't react, other than a pointed raise of his eyebrow. "Give Maddie a minute to speak to the girl," the older man said mildly.

Coop was poised on his toes, mind whirling with ways he could convince Belle. None that painted him in a pretty light.

"Besides, I'm not convinced you should marry a woman you just met," Doc went on.

"You did!" Coop threw the words at him, blood boiling.

Though the man didn't react, Coop still held the memory of the moments when Doc had punched him. It'd happened weeks ago, on a night when the good Doc had been lost in grief and emotion.

Now he simply watched Coop calmly. It couldn't be more obvious that love, marrying Maddie, had settled something inside the man.

Marriage seemed like such an easy answer. Belle needed protection from the man hunting her, from salacious gossip within the company, and from the wandering eyes of the more disreputable men among them. But Belle hadn't even considered a wagon train wedding before she'd stormed off. Sure, there were better prospects than him, but he was *here*, and he was *willing*.

"What's going on?" A new voice joined, coming closer.

A voice Coop well knew. His older brother, Leo.

Coop turned to start back after Belle. Heard the doc answer Leo. "Hollis just gave orders that Belle must marry to stay on the wagon train. Your brother is trying to convince her to say yes."

He registered Leo's angry grunt and heard the crunch of his brother's boots on the rocky ground. Following Coop.

Yet another sign of Coop's disfavor with his Maker.

The women had stopped walking at Maddie and the doc's wagon, where Belle was clambering up inside the conveyance. She disappeared inside the canvas cover.

And Coop turned to face his stubborn brother, knowing that Leo wouldn't walk away without words.

Looking at Leo was like peering in a looking glass. The same dark hair, the same nose, although Leo was clean shaven while Coop had two days of scruff on his chin.

Leo's expression was a thundercloud, and Coop braced for the blast he knew was coming.

"You can't marry that—"

"Girl," Coop interrupted, voice dangerous though quiet. He'd heard whispers from others in the company, derogatory words about her former profession, about the woman herself. He couldn't stand hearing it from his brother. "Girl or woman, that's the word you're looking for."

Because he'd also overheard a quiet sentence from Doc recently. *Not everyone chooses that life. Some women are forced into it.*

Coop didn't know Belle's story, how she'd ended up in a bordello and then escaped to the wagon train. But he wanted to. Just like he wanted to protect her from any cruel words that might be hurled at her.

Leo's eyes flashed with displeasure. Coop stood his ground.

"I forbid you to marry her." Now it was Leo's voice that carried a dangerous weight.

Coop's temper flared hotter than the wildfire the company had fought months ago. "You *forbid* me?"

Even as the familiar energy crackled through him—oh, he ached to throw a punch, to wipe that holier-than-thou expression from his brother's face—a visceral memory took hold of him.

Falling down that cave chute only two days ago, being in free-fall, trying to find the floor, trying to keep Belle from being injured. The feel of her sharp elbow and grappling hands as she'd tried to fight him off. She was so *slight*, like she'd been half-starved for years. And yet, so fierce. He'd felt the gouge of her fingers, the desperation in every movement as they'd taken that tumble together.

They'd been trapped in the cave overnight, walked and crawled for what seemed miles of tunnel before they'd found a half-buried exit.

He would never forget the stark fear in her voice in the darkness.

She'd been afraid of *him*, even though she hadn't needed to be. And if he had any chance of convincing her to marry him, to let him protect her, he didn't want to scare her worse.

Which meant he had to keep control of his temper. No matter how badly he wanted to slug his brother.

He took a breath that burned all the way down and didn't quench the fire burning inside him. Leo would never understand him. Never forgive him for what'd happened back in New Jersey.

But that couldn't matter in this moment.

He forced his voice to calm. "I'm not six years old anymore. I'm a man grown."

"You're acting like a youth," Leo argued, stepping into Coop's space. "Following a spur-of-the-moment whim—"

"It's not a whim." The truth of it hit Coop hard, eased his temper back a smidge more. The first moment he'd seen Belle, the earth had shifted beneath his feet. The air had felt different.

She mattered.

And after weeks of trying to befriend her, days when they'd been escaping the man stalking her through the wilderness, Coop was *this close* to having a real chance to make things work with her. He wouldn't let his brother cost him this chance.

"As I recall, you said I wasn't your brother any more." The words had cut when Leo had thrown them at Coop weeks ago, but now they were just a fact. Had to be. "So you don't have any standing to stop me."

Leo's jaw reddened beneath the tan earned by months on the trail. A muscle ticked in his cheek.

Coop waited several moments to see if he'd respond.

He didn't.

So Coop turned to Maddie's wagon, where Belle was climbing down. She'd changed dresses. From the plain, serviceable work dress Alice had given her to the threadbare gown with shiny fabric and a plunging neckline that she'd worn when she first came to the company.

Seeing her in that dress again made his stomach knot. She couldn't really mean to walk away from the wagons that meant safety?

"Do you really think you can be the husband she needs?" Leo's words were spoken quietly, but they carried. He must've meant them to.

And they cut.

Leo knew—most everyone knew—about the mill explosion back in New Jersey. That Coop had been responsible, though only he knew the truth of what'd happened that terrible night.

Coop was to blame, there was no doubt about that. He wasn't a good man. His family knew him best of all.

But Leo was wrong about this. Coop finally had something to fight for—Belle. She needed help. More than that, she needed someone on her side.

Why shouldn't it be him?

Maddie was speaking urgently as he approached. "...maybe it wouldn't be so bad."

"I won't marry *anyone*," Belle snapped.

Both women faced away from Coop, but they must've registered his approach, even if they hadn't acknowledged him.

Belle met Maddie's stare and something tiny softened in her expression. "I can't." The words seemed to beg Maddie to understand.

Belle held out a bundle of fabric—it must be the dress, along with the shawl Coop had given her anonymously—pushing it toward Maddie. "Can you give these back to Alice? Please?"

A cold breeze whispered through the woods nearby and Belle shivered.

That protective urge rose inside Coop, melding with frustration.

"She meant for you to keep that dress," he said, inserting himself into their conversation.

Maddie flicked a glance his way while Belle didn't acknowledge him at all. Was she embarrassed? Worried about his intentions? If he knew what was holding her back, he could find the right thing to say to ease her mind.

"What about Sarge?"

"*What about Sarge?*"

Those words had been reverberating through Belle for the past tumultuous minutes as she'd slipped out of the dress

Alice had given her and back into the low-cut dress she'd had on when she'd made her escape into the wilderness.

Now Maddie looked on with concerned eyes, Coop at her elbow. She was too aware of his presence, solid and warm in the chilly morning air. She couldn't look at him. Couldn't meet his eyes.

Around them, the company was stirring to life inside the circle of wagons. Someone called out about hitching the oxen. The scent of woodsmoke hung heavy as families doused their breakfast fires, the acrid smell mixing with the crisp mountain air. Belle's breath came out in small clouds. The chill bit through the threadbare shawl—meant to look pretty, not keep her warm. Her fingers twisted in the fabric and she tried to stifle a wish that she was back in Alice's borrowed clothing.

"You know he's out there watching and waiting for you." Coop's voice was low, urgent.

Belle's chest tightened. A visceral memory flashed through her mind—her friend's blood dripping off that knife blade, falling into the dirt in fat, dark drops. Pretty's hand flopping lifeless. Belle hadn't felt safe since she'd left the brothel.

But she hadn't felt safe there either.

She'd been terrified when she and Coop and Rob Braddock had been separated from the company. For three days the three of them had been alone in the wilderness. Sarge had come upon them. Rob had almost been killed.

Days ago, she and Coop had fallen into a deep cave in the mountain pass. Stranded in the dark overnight with no food, no fire, no light.

She couldn't remember a time when she had felt safe.

A wagon creaked somewhere behind her. Horses stamped and snorted, their breath steaming in the cold. Belle's hands started to shake.

"I promised myself I wouldn't let a man be in control of my life ever again." The words came out sharp, harder than she'd intended.

"Maybe it wouldn't be so bad."

The words were barely out of Coop's mouth before Belle turned on him. Her pulse hammered in her throat. She glared up at him, not caring that her voice would carry.

"Your own brother doesn't think you should marry me." She'd heard the argument from moments ago, over Maddie's soft-spoken words.

She saw a muscle tick in his jaw. The hard set of his mouth. He looked away for just a second, toward where someone was loading supplies into a wagon bed.

She never would have dared to speak to someone in the brothel like that. Would have kept her head down, her voice soft. But she couldn't seem to stop shaking, and she couldn't afford to show any weakness. Not now. Not when everything was unraveling.

That stubborn look she'd seen before crossed Coop's features.

Maddie's eyes went wide.

"I'm gonna excuse myself." As she walked away, her adopted sons Alex and Paul came running up, breathless and laughing. Their words tumbled over each other as they told Maddie about something gross that Tommy the dog had rolled in, their voices high and excited. Their chatter woke Jenny, who'd been asleep in the wagon. The baby's fussing carried on the morning air. Belle's stomach twisted with guilt. She'd taken care not to wake her.

Maddie glanced over her shoulder, her gaze flicking between Belle and Coop. "Maybe you two should take a walk."

Coop looked to Belle, quiet for a few seconds.

She gave a jerky nod.

They set off at a walk, skirting the inside edge of the circled wagons. People were rolling bedding, loading cookware, calling to their children. Outside the circled wagons, men paced with weapons in hand—on watch. Belle kept her eyes on the ground, aware of curious glances following them.

"We should stay inside the circle of wagons," Coop said quietly. "For safety."

She knew he meant Sarge. Always Sarge, lurking somewhere out there. Did his gun still have bullets? He'd sent several shots into the camp today.

They walked in silence for a moment, their footsteps crunching on the frost-stiffened grass. The mountains loomed around them, dark green slopes rising into gray clouds.

When he spoke again, Coop's voice was measured. Deliberate.

"I've got a quarter of that herd out there beyond the wagons coming to me when we get to Oregon. My portion." He turned his face, studied her as he kept speaking. "Just because we get married now doesn't mean we have to stay married. But if you agree to it, I'll give you half. It'll be a start for you."

She felt the weight of his expectant stare as her mind raced. Half the cattle. A way out. But married to him?

"How do you expect we'll get out of this marriage once we reach Oregon?" Belle's voice came out rougher than she'd intended. She cleared her throat. "It can't be much longer."

"I reckon it's gotta be against the law to force somebody into marriage." Coop's hands were shoved deep in his pockets as he walked. "Surely, we can get it annulled once we're settled in Oregon."

Belle hiked her chin up, trying to look braver than she felt. "What does that mean? Annulled?"

Color rose high on Coop's cheeks, visible even in the gray morning light. "Canceled."

Belle's brow furrowed. "I didn't know that was a thing."

Coop's blush deepened, color spreading down his neck. He looked away, toward where someone was yoking oxen to their wagon. When he spoke, his voice was quieter. "I've only heard of it done when the marriage wasn't consummated."

Belle's shock must have shown on her face because Coop ducked his head and rubbed the back of his neck with one hand. The gesture looked almost boyish, uncomfortable.

"I would never expect to take such liberties."

Belle didn't really know what to do with that. In her experience, men always expected something. Always took what they wanted. But Coop—he'd given her his gun in that cave. Had kept his hands careful and respectful even when they'd been pressed together for warmth in the darkness, trying to survive until morning.

She wrapped her arms tighter around herself inside the shawl.

"I know you and your brother don't get along." She kept

her voice even, trying to understand. "Why do you think you'll have a right to those cattle?"

Coop got a stricken look on his face, then his jaw set in that way she was beginning to recognize.

"I reckon he won't have a choice." His voice was tight with conviction. "I've worked my tail off to get them this far. And when we get to Oregon, I plan to take charge of what is rightly mine."

The determination in his voice was unmistakable. Belle studied his face—the set of his shoulders, the way his hands had formed into fists at his sides.

Around them, the camp continued its morning preparations. A child laughed somewhere. A woman called out about a missing bonnet. The smell of extinguished fires and damp earth filled the air.

Belle's mind couldn't grasp it. Half of a quarter of the herd. Those beasts were more money than she'd ever touched.

But it meant being tied to this man. Even if temporarily.

She thought about Pretty's lifeless hand. About Sarge's cold eyes. About the wilderness stretching between here and Oregon, full of dangers she couldn't even name.

And she thought about the alternative—being cast out of the wagon train. Alone.

Her hands started to shake again.

He was waiting for an answer.

It seemed she was out of choices.

Chapter Two

Coop watched Belle's face as she wrestled with his offer. The morning light caught the tension in her jaw, the way her hands wouldn't stop twisting in that threadbare shawl. She was trying so hard to be brave.

Half his cattle. It was a wild offer—Leo would have his hide for it—but seeing that flicker of hope in her eyes made it worth every head of livestock he'd worked to keep alive these past months.

Around them, wagon wheels creaked. Someone was whistling off-key.

Then the crack of gunfire split the morning air.

Coop's hand went to his revolver even as his eyes swept the circled wagons. Where—

Dust flew up from where a bullet had slammed into the ground near the Spencer family's wagon, maybe thirty yards away. Close enough to Belle's old position that his stomach dropped.

Belle was here, beside him, eyes wide with shock. But over there—

Ben, the little girl who played with Jenny nearly every day. She stood frozen near the wagon, her small face white with terror. Alex was there too, baby Jenny in his arms. Paul was nowhere Coop could see. Where was Maddie?

For one suspended heartbeat, nobody moved.

Then Belle's head whipped toward the children and Coop saw the stark fear wash over her features. Her whole body coiled like a spring.

She broke into a run.

"Shooter!" Coop's voice tore from his throat as he sprinted after her.

Around them, men shouted. Somewhere to his left, Gerry Bones—one of Leo's cowboys—yelled something about the ridge. But Coop's whole focus narrowed to Belle's flying skirts, to those children standing exposed and vulnerable.

Belle reached them first.

She scooped Alex and Jenny into a hug, pushing them behind the nearest wagon, turning her back toward where the shots had come from.

Ben stood frozen in place, eyes wide with terror. Coop pulled her around the edge of the wagon after Belle. Coop peered around the canvas, his eyes scanning the cliffs beyond the wagons. His heart slammed against his ribs hard enough to hurt.

A bullet whistled past his head, ripping the canvas. So close he felt the air move, felt the heat of it.

The slug punched into a nearby barrel with a sound like a fist hitting flesh. Wood splintered. Flour began trickling out through the fresh hole.

From her hiding place behind another wagon, Maddie watched with wide eyes. She wouldn't be able to reach the kids.

"We've got to get to better cover." Coop kept his voice steady despite the adrenaline singing through every nerve.

Ben was sobbing, her shoulders shaking.

Belle met his gaze, eyes wide with fear.

More shouts erupted around them. He recognized voices—the men Owen and Hollis had tasked with hunting down Sarge if he showed himself again.

"He's up in that outcropping!"

Coop leaned out from behind the wagon, gaze snapping up to the cliffside again. His gut knotted.

Last night, sitting around the campfire with some of the cowboys after everyone else had bedded down, Rusty had pointed at that very vista.

"I don't like the look of that spot. Somebody could see straight down into camp from up there."

Lucky had scoffed. *"You think that Sarge is gonna be able to climb up there? If he's hurt like Braddock claims?"*

Coop had been busy thinking of the day ahead. He should've paid better attention.

Like Rusty had said, from that vantage point, Sarge would have a clear view down into the entire circle of wagons. So far, his shots had gone wide, and Coop knew Leo's men would be going after him now. They'd try to trap him up on that ridge. But they'd have to find a careful way up or risk putting themselves right in his sights. It might make him more desperate.

Another shot cracked.

Ben cried out from where she was huddled into Coop—a small, terrified sound that cut straight through him.

They'd taken cover behind the nearest wagon, but it wasn't enough. The angle was wrong. When the bullet hit, it splintered the wooden side. Shards flew. The whole structure shuddered.

Belle held Jenny close, the baby's wails muffled against her shoulder. She looked at the children—taking stock, making sure they were whole—then looked directly at Coop.

Her eyes were too dark. Too determined. He knew that look.

"I have to do something." Her voice came out tight, barely above a whisper. "It's me he wants. Maybe if I—" She swallowed hard. "Maybe I can run off into the woods. It'll take him a while to come down off that ridge. I can outrun him."

Horror crashed through Coop's chest.

"No." He bit out.

"Do you have a better idea?"

"Any idea is better than that. I won't give him a chance to get to you." His mind raced, searching desperately for options.

Alex was trying to calm Jenny, reaching for the crying baby with hands that shook. The boy was putting on a brave face, trying so hard to be strong. But he was terrified. Ben was too.

Coop's gaze swept their surroundings. They were pinned behind this wagon—too exposed. They needed a way out. Fast.

"I wish we could be in one of those caves right now." Ben's small voice cut through Coop's racing thoughts.

Caves. Hiding places.

His attention snapped to the rocky outcropping maybe thirty yards away—not the cliff Sarge was perched on, but a jumble of boulders near the tree line on the opposite side. If he could get Belle and the kids behind those rocks, they'd have better protection.

The problem was the stretch of open ground between here and there.

"It's me that he wants." Belle's voice again, quieter this time but no less determined.

Coop's focus shifted back to her. She'd gone pale, but her jaw was set in that stubborn way he was coming to know.

Then he saw it.

A broom, leaning against the inside of the wagon they were huddled behind.

A crazy idea sparked in his mind. Desperate. But maybe—

"If we can use this broom to trick Sarge into thinking you're running that direction—" He reached for it, his brain working through the mechanics even as he spoke. "—he's gonna take a shot. It'll be a few seconds before he can reload. While all that's happening, you and the kids are gonna run to those rocks over there."

Belle's eyebrows drew together. Skeptical.

"Why would he shoot at a stupid broom?" Alex piped up, his young voice sharp with fear and confusion.

Coop's pulse hammered as the plan crystallized. "What if you take off that dress and we rig it on the broom to look like it's you? It might work for a few seconds."

Belle's eyes went wide as saucers. "I can't run around naked."

A smile twitched at his lips, despite the danger.

"You can wear my clothes." He was already working the buttons on his shirt, fingers clumsy with haste. "I've got long underwear on."

Another shot rang out. This one slapped into the wagon bed.

Everyone flinched. Ben whimpered.

Coop's hands stilled for just a second as he looked at the little girl. Fat tears rolled down her cheeks, and something in his chest cracked at the sight.

Belle's lips pressed into a thin line. She looked at Ben, at Alex trying so hard to soothe the crying baby, at the chaos around them.

Then she gave a single, reluctant nod.

Coop stopped unbuttoning halfway and shucked his shirt over his head. The morning air was cold through his union suit, raising goosebumps along his arms.

"We'll close our eyes," Alex offered, his voice trying for steady and almost making it.

They were huddled close in the cramped space behind the wagon—close enough that Coop could feel the shift of movement when Belle took his shirt. Could sense when she slipped it over her head.

He focused on working his way out of his pants, keeping his long underwear firmly in place. The rustle of fabric and Ben's soft cries filled the small space between them.

She pressed the dress into his hands a moment later. Their fingers brushed—just for a heartbeat—and then she was taking his pants, clutching them against her chest.

There was a beat of awkwardness. Strange and charged in a way that made Coop's throat tight despite the circumstances.

He looked at the worn fabric in his hands. The dress she'd been wearing when she first came to the company. That shiny, threadbare thing that marked her past.

"You should burn this old thing." The words came out before he thought them through.

Then, as determination filled him: "This isn't who you are anymore."

Belle looked at him like she didn't understand. Her eyes held his for a long moment, something vulnerable flickering there before she looked away.

No time for this now.

Coop grabbed the broom and started rigging the dress over the bristled end. His hands moved fast, tying fabric, creating something that might—if Sarge was far enough away and desperate enough—look like a running woman.

He gathered the children and Belle into a tight huddle.

"You might only have a few seconds." He looked at Alex first, then Ben, trying to put as much confidence in his voice as he could muster. "I want you to run the fastest you've ever run before. Get all the way behind those rocks. Don't stop. Don't look back."

He reached for Belle's elbow—an instinct to reassure her, to connect—but the moment his fingers brushed her arm, she flinched.

Coop's hand dropped immediately, something cold settling in his stomach. "Are you okay?"

She nodded. Just once. Quick and jerky. "What about you? You'll be stuck over here."

The worry in her voice did something inside his chest.

"We only have to buy a little time." Coop made himself

sound more confident than he felt. "The men are after Sarge. He's going to have to leave or get caught."

He moved to one end of the wagon with his makeshift decoy, the broom awkward in his hands. Belle and the kids shifted to the opposite end, closest to the rocks.

Coop caught Belle's eye across the space.

She looked like she didn't believe this would work—like she thought they were all about to die—but she crouched low, ready to run, with both children pressed close against her sides and Jenny to her chest.

He winked.

"Three." Coop's voice was barely audible over the pounding of his own heart. "Two. One."

He thrust the dress past the edge of the wagon, moving the broom in an arc like someone running.

The shot came so fast it made him jerk.

From the corner of his eye, Coop saw them go. Belle with Jenny clutched tight—his shirt hanging loose on her frame, the pants bunched and rolled at her ankles. Alex and Ben, their small legs pumping, arms swinging.

Running for their lives.

Coop's mind automatically went through the motions of reloading a rifle. Pull back the bolt. Reach for the cartridge. Slide it home. Lock it in place. Aim.

How long? Five seconds? Seven? *God, please let it be enough—*

He barely thought the desperate prayer before the children reached the jutting rocks and disappeared behind them like rabbits diving into a burrow.

Belle was right behind, moving fast despite the ill-fitting clothes.

Another shot cracked out just as she slipped behind the stone outcropping.

The bullet pinged harmlessly off rock, ricocheting away with a high whine.

They were safe.

Coop's breath left him in a rush that made him dizzy. His hands were shaking—from adrenaline or relief, he couldn't tell. Maybe both.

He'd done it. Come up with a spur-of-the-moment plan. And it'd worked.

Coop stayed low behind the wagon, still clutching the broom with Belle's old dress tied to it. The fabric fluttered in the breeze, a ghost of the woman who'd worn it.

His heart was still hammering. But Belle and the children were safe. Hidden behind solid rock, protected.

That was all that mattered.

Twenty minutes later, Belle's hands wouldn't stop shaking.

She sat behind Jason and Maddie's wagon, tucked into the narrow space between the wagon bed and a stack of supply crates. Her knees were drawn up tight to her chest, arms wrapped around them. Coop's clothes hung loose on her frame—the shirt swallowing her shoulders, the pants bunched and rolled at her ankles. The fabric smelled like leather and woodsmoke and something else she couldn't name.

She liked how the clothes covered her completely. How you couldn't tell her shape beneath all that excess fabric.

Jason knelt beside her, his medicine bag open at his feet.

Maddie had the kids huddled together nearby, calming them as she checked them for bumps and bruises.

Coop sat on an overturned crate a few feet away, staring at something in the distance. Someone had given him a slicker, but he had unbuttoned the top of his union suit and his bare chest was on display. A trickle of blood stained his collar, dark against the pale fabric of his undershirt. Doc had taken a look at Coop first and determined he was only scraped and not in need of patching up.

Doc's hands were gentle as he examined the side of her face, but Belle still had to force herself not to pull away.

"You've got a big splinter lodged just here. Almost a log." His fingers probed carefully behind her left ear. She felt a tug of pain and then a low throb. "There. Got it. But you're going to need a few stitches."

Belle hadn't even realized she was hurt. There'd been the crack of gunfire, the children's terrified faces, the desperate run to the rocks. Everything after that was a blur.

Alex was jabbering to his older brother, who'd been out of the line of fire.

"Belle was braver than Maddie when she went up against that bear," Alex said, his voice high and excited as he bounced on his toes nearby. "Or—or maybe braver than Doc when he rescued us from the wildfire!"

Doc shook his head, a slight smile tugging at his mouth as he threaded a needle.

Belle didn't feel brave. All she'd felt was overwhelming terror that the children were going to be hurt because of her. Sarge wanted her dead and didn't care who got caught in the crossfire.

Around them, the camp was organized chaos. After the

shooting stopped, Hollis had given the order to move out as quickly as possible. He wanted distance between the caravan and that dangerous outcropping.

How could they just... go on? Was she the only one who was frozen?

"Hollis and the captains are making plans," Doc said quietly, as if he'd heard her unspoken question. "Trying to keep everybody as safe as they can while we move forward."

Belle's stomach churned.

"You still have my gun." Coop's voice startled her. She'd almost forgotten he was there, he'd been so quiet.

Belle's hand went automatically to the pocket of the oversized pants. Felt the heavy weight of the revolver there. She'd kept it close ever since the cave, even switched it to the pants pocket during her quick change.

"I don't know how to use it." The admission scraped her throat raw.

Coop turned his head slightly, speaking over his shoulder. "Never been taught to shoot?"

"No."

"Nothing hard about it." His voice was matter-of-fact, no judgment in it. "I can teach you."

The thought of holding that gun, of pointing it at Sarge, made her hands shake worse.

"This is going to sting." Doc said. From the corner of her eye, she saw him reach for her.

Before she could blink, her mind registered his movement as a fist flying in her direction.

She jerked, ducking away. Her fingers dug into her knees through the thick fabric of Coop's pants.

And then she went still, realizing that her mind had played a trick on her. Doc hadn't been trying to hit her.

Doc watched her with brows slightly raised.

And Coop had gone very still.

Of course he'd noticed. Something flickered across his expression before his features smoothed into careful blankness.

She did her best to relax the tense set of her shoulders but couldn't quite uncoil the way her body had gone rigid. "You can go ahead."

"Hold still." Doc's voice was gentle as his fingers moved to Belle's jaw, tilting her head slightly to get better access to the cut. She flinched before she could stop herself.

"Sorry." The word came out automatically, shame flooding through her. "I know you're only trying to help."

"You're doing fine," Jason said, his voice carrying that same gentle patience. She felt the first prick of his needle.

She couldn't seem to stop her body from reacting. Every touch made her want to pull away, to run. Her hands were shaking again.

"I never had a choice," she heard herself say, the words flowing so quickly she couldn't seem to stop them. "About who was allowed to touch me. And now I can't seem to stop flinching away."

Doc's hands stilled for just a moment. When he spoke again, his voice was understanding.

"Your body is only trying to protect you." He resumed his work, movements steady and sure. "Your brain knows what you shouldn't have had to bear. Touch from someone who's being cruel. Using you."

She bit down hard on the inside of her cheek to keep tears at bay. Her throat ached with the effort of holding back.

Aware of Coop watching, she stared at the collar of Doc's shirt as he worked.

It didn't take long for Doc to put in three stitches, then he was dabbing the spot with a rag soaked in disinfectant and standing to his full height. "Be right back," he murmured before he moved to where Maddie stood, yards away, Jenny on her hip. He smiled, warm and soft, reached out to touch his wife's hand, just for a moment.

They were obviously in love.

Belle glanced away. Her gaze collided with Coop's stare. He'd abandoned his crate and moved to stand closer to her, arms crossed over his chest.

"Did you say no to marrying me because you're waiting to fall in love with somebody?" Coop's voice was quieter now. Careful.

Belle's chin hiked up. "I won't fall in love."

His brows scrunched together, confusion crossing his features.

The words came out before she could stop them. "I don't have it in me. I can't love anybody."

Coop looked at her for a long moment, something thoughtful in his expression. Then he tipped his head toward Alex, who stood next to Maddie and was attempting to play pat-a-cake with baby Jenny. The baby was giggling, reaching for the boy's nose.

"You love those kids," Coop said.

Belle started to shake her head, but he kept going.

"You must. Because you were willing to protect them with your life."

The truth rose inside her, along with a heavy dose of panic. "It's not the same."

"All right." Coop's voice stayed level, measured. "We can take that out of the discussion then. This would be a business arrangement between us. Nothing more."

A business arrangement.

Belle's throat felt tight.

She hadn't realized Doc had come back for his bag until he spoke.

"If that's what you plan to do, I would keep quiet about it. If Hollis or your brother hears you're treating marriage like a business arrangement, they won't like it." He snapped the bag closed and picked it up.

The unspoken implication hung in the air—Coop and Belle might be forced out of the wagon train.

As Doc walked away, Coop's jaw set in his stubborn way. But he didn't take back his offer.

"I need to go out and ride with the cattle." Coop dropped his arms to his sides, rolled his shoulders like he was testing for injury. "Make sure they didn't scatter too far during all the commotion."

His stare intensified.

"Are we in agreement?" His voice was softer than before. "About the arrangement?"

Belle's hands twisted in the fabric of his shirt that she wore. She thought about Sarge in those hills. About being cast out of the wagon train with nowhere to go, wilderness stretching in every direction.

She thought about Coop giving her his gun in the cave. About him stepping between her and the shooter this morning as bullets flew. About the way he'd looked at her old dress and said *This isn't who you are anymore.*

She didn't know how to be anything else. The last four years of her life, she'd done everything she had to do to survive. She didn't know how to be normal anymore.

But maybe this arrangement could buy her time to figure it out. Keep her safe until the company reached Oregon.

"Yes." The word came out barely above a whisper. "We're in agreement."

Something shifted in Coop's expression. Not quite a smile, but close.

"Tonight then," he said.

"Mr. Smith and Lucky lost his trail," Owen said, voice tired. "It's like he disappeared. Tracks are gone."

Leo stood with arms crossed, watching Owen give his report. They'd gathered near Hollis's wagon—Leo, Hollis, Owen, and two other wagon captains. The evening light was fading. Shadows stretching long across the circled wagons. A small fire had been lit. Abigail moved quietly around the fire, checking supplies for supper. She caught Hollis's eye and he gave her a subtle nod—he wouldn't be much longer. The quiet understanding between them was something Leo noticed more and more these days. Hollis had changed since marrying Abigail—still gruff, still a firm leader, but with an ease about him that hadn't been there before.

"You want me to send some men back out?" Owen asked.

Hollis shook his head gravely. "Better if we scout out ahead. Find a safe place to make camp tomorrow."

Leo made a frustrated sound.

Hollis's gaze flicked to him. "You got something to add, Spencer?"

Leo shook his head.

But inside, the thought burned: They'd be better off if that saloon girl hadn't snuck into one of the wagons.

A madman was chasing her. Shooting into their company. Putting families at risk. Women. Children. All because Belle had brought her past with her.

Leo wasn't heartless. The girl had suffered. He understood that. But she'd caused trouble for the company. Trouble for his family. And now Coop was about to make it permanent.

Hollis dismissed the other captains with a nod. "Spencer, stay."

The other men filed off into the growing darkness. Owen shot Leo a look before he walked away. Something between concern and warning.

Leo ignored it.

Darkness was falling properly now. The deep blue sky fading to black. Campfires flickered to life across the company. The sounds of evening—voices, laughter, the clank of cookware—drifted on the cold air.

Hollis squatted in front of the fire and reached for a stick to stir up the embers. Fed some more kindling to the flames.

"How can one man disappear in the wilderness?" Hollis muttered. He rubbed the back of his neck in a frustrated motion.

Leo watched the fire dance. "I don't want you to go through with the ceremony."

The words came out harder than he'd intended. But he didn't retract them.

Hollis didn't look up. Just shook his head. Fed another stick to the flames. Then he stood.

"That's not up to you," Hollis said. His voice was quiet but firm. "Your brother is determined to marry that girl. And then she'll be under the protection of the wagon train."

"That madman shot straight into the company today," Leo said. His hands fisted at his sides. "He could've killed—"

"Would you rather me put your brother out in the wild alone?" Hollis interrupted. He looked at Leo directly. "Send him off with no protection? No support?"

Leo's back teeth ground together.

"If he's choosing to marry her," Leo said, each word clipped, "then let him put himself in danger. Not all the rest of us."

Hollis shook his head. "You don't really mean that."

For a moment, the memory of Ma on her deathbed flashed through Leo's mind. The promise she'd extracted from him.

Leo's hands fisted at his sides. He wanted to argue until Hollis agreed with him. Coop needed someone to set him straight, and he'd been at odds with Leo for so long that nothing he said mattered anymore. But maybe Hollis could scare some sense into him.

"You should go check on your wife," Hollis said. A clear dismissal. "She seemed upset when I saw her this morning."

Hollis wasn't going to listen, either.

Leo turned on his heel. As he walked away, he glanced back to see Hollis settling by the fire, Abigail handing him a tin cup. She said something low that made the wagonmaster's weathered face soften into a smile. Even Hollis had found happiness on this trail.

As Leo strode through camp, seething, his boots hit the ground hard. Each step a release of frustration he couldn't voice.

Around him, families gathered. Children played. The normal rhythms of life on the trail.

But nothing felt normal for Leo. He felt off-balance. Like the world was tilting and Leo was the only one trying to hold it steady.

He wished he'd never made that promise to Ma. Yet he didn't know how he could've refused her. Not when she'd understood that this was the end, that she didn't have any more time on this earth. He could still feel her hand clasping his with all the strength she had left.

He would've promised her anything in that moment. So he'd promised to watch over his younger brothers. To keep their family together.

She couldn't have known then what her promise would cost him.

He was bone-deep exhausted from carrying weight that never got lighter. Collin had grown into a man Ma would've been proud of. Alice was the peacekeeper of the siblings and had become a responsible, kind woman who was now a wife. She'd make a good mother someday.

Where had things gone wrong with Coop?

He didn't seem to appreciate that Leo had given up his entire life back in New Jersey, even his dreams of traveling, of seeing Europe or Alaska. That Leo bore the burden of keeping their family fed and safe—all because of Coop, who only wanted to seek the next thrill. Carouse. Box. Drink.

Leo had sacrificed everything. Where was the respect he was due?

Coop continued to make messes. Left Leo to clean them up.

He didn't have any answers by the time he reached his own camp. Evangeline was there with Sara. The little girl sat at a makeshift table Evangeline had formed from a crate, eating dinner. Evangeline was helping her.

"There's stew in the pot," Evangeline said when she saw Leo.

"I'm not hungry." The words came out sharp.

Something flickered in Evangeline's eyes. Hurt, maybe.

"I think we should talk about—"

"If this is about Coop," Leo cut her off, "I refuse to go to that tawdry wedding. And you shouldn't go either."

Sara babbled happily, oblivious to the tension crackling between her parents.

Evangeline's expression turned wary. "Have you talked to Alice? Or Collin?"

A storm inside him churned. Rising. "There's nothing to talk about. He's making a mistake. He'll ruin his life. If he doesn't end up getting shot."

Evangeline's lips pinched together. She turned to Sara. The little girl had made a mess with her stew. Bits of carrot and potato smeared on her face. Her hands were sticky.

Evangeline used the hem of her apron to clean Sara's hands and then shooed the little girl from her seat. Sara scrambled down and ran straight to Leo.

She threw herself against his leg, chubby arms grabbing his pant leg.

Leo was so lost in his frustration at all of it that he barely put his hand on her head.

"I'll come tuck you in later," he said.

He sent Sara back to Evangeline with a gentle push.

Evangeline frowned. Was that a worry line between her brows?

Hollis had mentioned seeing her upset this morning. Leo had been upset, too, after the dangerous shootout.

Evangeline swept Sara up into her arms. There was something mulish in her expression.

"I really need to talk to you." She wasn't going to drop this conversation.

Leo shook his head. "I can't talk about Coop anymore. I've got to set some men on watch."

He turned and walked away without looking back.

Behind him, Evangeline exhaled softly. Murmured something to Sara. His daughter's voice asked a question he couldn't make out.

He should be enjoying a quiet night with his family. But he couldn't.

Because of Coop.

Chapter Three

"I bet she's in Maddie's wagon."

"Hiding?"

Evening was falling and long shadows made it hard to see inside the wagon with the canvas cover pulled tight. Belle registered the two women's voices—voices she knew, voices that continued conversing in low tones just outside the wagon—but kept up her stubborn attempt to push the needle and thread through a tear in the satin dress: the only property Belle had to her name. She'd been attempting to repair the gown for over an hour.

And it was hopeless. Completely hopeless.

It wasn't her terrible sewing skills.

It was the fact that the dress had never been meant for the kind of wear it had been subjected to. After she'd escaped the bordello, Belle had spent almost two weeks following the wagon train on foot through treacherous terrain, hiding in empty wagons when she could find one, stealing scraps of food. It was a wonder Maddie had been able to tell she was a woman, and not a wild animal, that first night she'd been discovered in the woods.

Belle pushed the memories away with the same fierce efficiency as she used to bite through the thread. She stowed the needle and tucked the hopeless gown between two crates. Useless to try and repair it when the fabric was disintegrating in her hands.

She'd climbed back into Maddie's wagon, still wearing Coop's clothes, as the company had pulled out. She'd needed the safety of the enclosed space, the canvas walls between her and the rest of the world. But she couldn't hide forever.

The hours had ticked away and now it surely must be time for her to get married.

She pulled back the canvas and glimpsed Coop's sister, Alice, and the woman Belle knew was named Rachel. Rachel had a little baby swaddled around her body with a blanket, the infant's face barely visible in the folds of fabric. The sight knotted Belle's stomach.

Belle didn't greet them as she clambered down from the wagon, her movements jerky and awkward in the oversized clothes.

She couldn't help looking around. Checking the tree line. The shadows between wagons. Sarge had shot right into camp this morning. Now every sound made her jump.

Rachel caught her glances and said quietly, "Three of the men tracked Sarge into the wilderness but lost him. Hollis feels certain they'll close in soon."

The words should have been comforting.

They weren't.

Alice added, "There are other men on guard now. Hollis

specifically looked for a place to camp out in the open, where it will be impossible for Sarge to sneak up on us."

Their voices were gentle. Like they were trying to calm a spooked horse. Belle recognized the tone. She'd heard it before, back at the brothel, when a drunken man needed to be talked down from the edge of the roof.

But she didn't understand why they were using it on her. What they wanted from her.

Rachel extended the hand not cradling her baby. "I'm Rachel. I don't believe we've been properly introduced."

Alice looked surprised. "You two haven't met?"

"Felicity and Evangeline would have come to help, but they didn't want to overwhelm you," Rachel went on.

Belle stared at Rachel's outstretched hand. A handshake meant—what? Agreement? Connection? She didn't know the rules of polite society. Not anymore. Slowly, she reached out and let her fingers brush Rachel's palm. The briefest touch before pulling back.

When Belle still didn't say anything, Rachel murmured, "You've been cooped up in that wagon for weeks." *Hiding.* She didn't say it aloud.

Belle had known it was wrong to steal food. She hadn't had a choice.

"That's over now," Alice said, voice matter-of-fact.

Belle's throat felt tight. These women knew what she was. What she had been. Everyone on the wagon train knew. She'd heard the whispers, seen the way people looked at her, or pointedly didn't look at her.

Alice's smile, a little too bright, somehow cut worse than the whispers from strangers. She held up a pail of water and a rag. "There's probably not time to visit the creek for a proper bath, but if you want to wash up before—" She paused, seemed to catch herself. "Before we go meet Hollis, you can use this." She produced a small sliver of soap from her pocket.

Rachel offered a folded dress, the fabric a soft brown. "And we thought you might need this. One dress isn't enough."

Belle didn't take the clothing. Gifts meant obligation. What did Rachel want?

"I can help you take it in or adjust the hem later on," Alice added. "If you'd like."

Belle didn't know what to make of the two of them. Their kindness felt like a trap. Like they wanted something from her, but she couldn't figure out what.

Alice said gently, "You'll want to freshen up a bit before the ceremony, won't you?"

The ceremony. Marriage. To Coop.

Belle's stomach twisted. *I won't go.*

But "Did Coop put you up to this?" was what came out of her mouth instead.

The women exchanged glances.

"Here." Alice held out the water and soap. "At least wash your face and hands. You'll feel better."

Would she? Belle doubted anything would make her feel better. But she took the offerings, dipped the rag in the cool water. The soap smelled like lye and something else. Lavender, maybe. She scrubbed at her hands, her face, the back of her neck. The water turned gray almost immediately.

"Do you want to change into the dress?" Rachel asked. "We can turn our backs."

Alice pushed the dress at her even though Belle hesitated. "Take it." Her tone brooked no argument.

"You're going to be family now. Family helps each other," Alice said.

Family. As if that solved it all.

Belle's immediate instinct was refusal. She'd had a family once. Lost them. She didn't know how to be family anymore.

Except she couldn't think about that. Wouldn't let herself remember the before times.

She scrubbed her neck with the rag.

She could still say no. Refuse to go through with it. Everything Coop had promised her earlier played through her mind. What would it be like to stand inside a log cabin, to close and lock the door? To choose who she let inside her own house? She could choose to keep *everyone* out.

The splash of water startled her out of that thought. She forced herself to think about the vows she'd be expected to speak. She was meant to bind herself to Coop. He'd promised to cancel the marriage—but when had a man ever kept his promise? Never. And what would he expect from her in the days until they reached Oregon?

Belle's hands started to shake.

Half his cattle. She pushed the thought forward.

He'd promised her half his herd. It was more money than she'd seen change hands at the saloon. Real independence. A new life for herself—

The thought of it was breathtaking and terrifying in the same measure.

She had to try. And if Coop backed out on the deal, she could slip away. Run. Once they reached a place with more people, more options. She'd survived worse. She could survive this.

As she plopped the rag back into the pail, Rachel's husband came walking past, stopped when he saw them. "You ladies about ready? They're waiting."

Alice and Rachel shooed him away with fluttering hands.

Owen tipped his hat and moved off, but not before Belle caught the curious, measuring, glance he threw her way.

"Would you like me to put up your hair?" Alice asked.

Belle's hand went automatically to her hair. It hung loose and tangled down her back. Her hair had been her one source of pride. The other girls had been jealous of the dark tresses. But she'd been in hiding, on the run for weeks. No comb had touched it. It was a tangled mess.

"I—" Belle's voice stuck.

But Alice had already pulled a comb from her pocket. "Just let me work some of the tangles out at least."

Before Belle could refuse, Alice was behind her, gently drawing the comb through Belle's hair. Rachel's baby started fussing and she walked in a slow circle, swaying back and forth.

Belle stood frozen as Alice worked on her hair. The comb caught on a knot and Belle flinched, but Alice murmured an apology and worked more carefully. Her gentle touch reminded Belle of a long ago time. Of those locked-away memories.

Her chest felt tight again.

"Coop's a good man," Alice said. "I know he doesn't always show it, but he is. He thinks outside the box. Can always find a solution to any problem."

Belle had seen the real Coop during her days of hiding and spying. Alice was generous in her view of her brother.

"He's been good with the children," Alice continued. "Protective of them. And he's done a fine job taking care of the cattle these past months." Alice's hand swept Belle's hair to one side of her neck. "Almost done," she muttered.

Belle still didn't say anything.

"It's clear he's smitten with you," Alice said, clear affection in her voice.

Smitten. Belle didn't want to think about that. Coop claimed to want a business arrangement.

"Does Coop drink?"

The words rushed out before Belle could stop them. She thought about the night she'd found him in the creek, passed out drunk, nearly drowned.

Alice's hands dropped from Belle's hair.

The silence stretched. Alice shifted to Belle's side.

Her lips were pressed into a thin line—the first crack in her cheerful facade. "Coop has his demons." Her voice was quieter now. Honest. "But I know he's trying to overcome them."

Belle had her own demons. A whole lifetime of them.

"I think the men are ready," Rachel said, her voice cutting through the sudden tension. "They're motioning for us to join them."

Alice stepped back as Belle wrapped her shawl tight around her shoulders. One hand went to the knife in her pocket. The familiar weight steadied her slightly.

"Come on," Alice said gently, and started toward the men.

Belle followed, each step feeling like walking toward a

cliff edge. Rachel fell into step beside her, and Belle was aware of the women flanking her. Like guards. Or maybe like friends, though Belle didn't know what that felt like anymore.

There were more people waiting than she'd expected.

The wagon master stood at the center, holding some kind of book. Coop's twin brother stood beside him. August and Owen were there too. The women—Felicity, Evangeline holding her little girl. Ben, the girl who belonged to Felicity, clinging to her ma's skirts.

Too many people. Too many eyes.

Coop's back was to her as she approached. Then he turned, and his eyes found her face.

Something warm flickered in his gaze. Something that made Belle's stomach knot uncomfortably. She ducked her head. Felt Alice standing at her back. Keeping her trapped? Or there for support?

Belle went to stand beside Coop on legs that didn't feel steady.

The warmth in his expression made her feel exposed. Like he could see straight through her to all the broken, ruined parts.

The wagon master cleared his throat. His gaze landed on Belle, and she saw resignation in the set of his jaw.

"Miss," he said. Then paused. "Are you sure you want to go through with this?"

Coop tensed beside her.

Belle's throat was too tight to speak. *Think of the cattle.* She gave a single, jerky nod.

Hollis studied her for a long moment. Then: "I'm going to need your name for the ceremony."

Her name. *Belle.* The word, her name stuck in her throat.

She'd been Belle for four years. But before that—

She'd been a girl with a different name, a different life. The men at the brothel—Thaddeus, Virgil, Sarge, others—had taken everything from her. Her freedom. Her innocence.

Her name was the one thing she'd kept.

Even now a flicker of memory tickled her brain. A woman's voice calling out for her in the distant past. Belle refused to let the memory surface.

That girl was gone.

"Belle." The word came out barely above a whisper.

Tonight, Belle would become Mrs. Coop Spencer.

Take a new name.

For better or worse.

"I suppose you're going to tell me I'm making a bad decision."

Coop didn't look up as Collin approached where he knelt at the creek bank, wringing out his shirt for the second time. Water dripped between his fingers, darkened by the day's accumulation of sweat and dust and dried blood from the cut on his neck. He used the damp fabric to wipe his chest, beneath his arms, the back of his neck where the grime seemed to settle deepest.

The shirt would need a proper washing later. For now, it would have to do.

His fresh shirt—the only other one he owned—lay spread over a nearby bush. He'd debated taking time for a shave but decided against it. The wagons were circling up, the last of them rolling into position. Gerry Bones, Rusty, and Matt were on watch with the cattle, the herd settled in a small grassy area for the night.

It was only a matter of minutes before he needed to show up in front of Hollis.

To marry Belle.

His hand went unconsciously to his pocket, felt the band of metal there. The silver ring. A blip of uncertainty. He'd made a handshake deal with Larson, one of the other men in Hollis's company. Until now, Coop hadn't had any dealings with the man, though he knew his reputation. Coop had asked for a loan. He'd taken the money from Larson now, and would pay the man back once they reached Oregon. Somehow. He hadn't quite figured that part out yet.

He could've asked Leo for money. But he knew his brother would refuse.

And Coop wanted that ring for Belle. A visual reminder that she was his wife.

He'd also secured enough funds for the other needs Belle might have during these last few days on the trail.

He'd make it work. Figure out how to pay Larson back.

The pause between him and Collin had lasted long enough that Coop finally shot his brother a look.

Collin stared back with steady eyes that were a mirror of Coop's own.

"Well?" Coop demanded. He dropped the wet shirt on a rock and reached for the dry one. "You got something to say, say it."

"What would I say?"

"That I'm making a mistake." Coop shoved his arms

through the sleeves, started working the buttons. His fingers felt clumsy. "That I don't know her well enough to marry her. That I'm not—" He bit off the words, jaw clenching.

Collin swept his hat off his head and raised one eyebrow. "That you're not what?"

Heat crawled up Coop's neck. "That I'm gonna fail at this like I fail at everything else."

"Do you think that?"

"I think—" Coop's fingers stilled on a button. "I think Leo sure believes it."

Collin could've argued. He didn't.

"She needs protection," Coop said, going back to his shirt buttons. "She needs someone to stand between her and Sarge, between her and—and everything else."

"And that's you?"

Coop's hands formed into fists before he deliberately relaxed them. "Why not me?"

Collin's expression didn't change. "That's what I'm asking. Why you?"

"Because I'm here." Coop grabbed his hat from where he'd set it on a stump, finger-combed his hair back. "Because I'm willing. Because—"

He stopped. The words caught in his throat, sharp-edged and true.

"Because the first time I saw her, something shifted." His voice came out quieter than he'd intended. "Like the world tilted and suddenly everything made sense. Like I'm meant to be with her."

Collin's eyebrow twitched upward again.

Coop shoved his hat on his head, pulled it low. "I aim to prove to her that I can be the kind of husband she needs.

And I'll prove to Leo too that I am more of a man than he thinks I am."

He felt Collin study him as he moved to pick up the sopping wet shirt.

Collin spoke, measured and careful: "I think you can do it."

"But?" Coop prompted, hearing the edge in his own voice.

"But nothing." Collin's expression stayed neutral. "If you say you're going to be the husband she needs, I believe you'll try."

Try.

Not succeed.

Coop's jaw tightened. He turned away from his brother, started walking back toward camp. Collin fell into step beside him, and Coop was aware of the loaded silence between them.

Campfires flickered to life as families settled in for the night. Children's voices carried on the evening air, along with the distant lowing of cattle and the clink of silverware on dishes. Normal sounds. Safe sounds.

Except Sarge was still out there somewhere in the darkness.

Hollis stood waiting near the center of the wagon circle, positioned behind one of the wagons where they'd have some shelter from view. Owen and August stood nearby, along with Coop's sisters-in-law. His family had gathered to witness this moment.

But Leo wasn't there.

Coop's teeth ground together. Anger stirred in his gut

like someone poking at dying embers, trying to bring the flames back to life.

Leo had made his opinion clear. Thought this was another one of Coop's impulsive, reckless decisions that would end badly.

Collin's hand landed on Coop's shoulder, squeezed once. Then his brother leaned close and whispered, "Here comes Belle."

Coop shoved the anger down deep, buried it where it couldn't touch this moment. He turned.

And his breath caught.

Belle walked toward them, flanked by Alice and Rachel. She wore a simple brown dress and her hair had been pinned up. The evening light caught on her pale face, making her look almost ethereal. Fragile.

Their eyes met.

Something visceral moved through Coop's chest. An echo of that feeling he'd tried to describe to Collin. Recognition. Rightness.

It didn't matter what Leo thought. Didn't matter that Coop had a history of letting people down.

Belle was different.

You're gonna fail her, a voice whispered in the back of his mind. *You always fail.*

Coop's jaw set. Not this time.

He'd prove he was the man Belle needed him to be.

She reached the small gathering, and Coop saw her hands twisting in her shawl. Alice stepped back, giving Belle space to stand beside Coop, and for a moment they just looked at each other.

Her gaze darted away, landing on Hollis, on the book in his hands, on anything but Coop.

"Miss," Hollis said. "I'll need your name for the ceremony."

Belle went very still. She hesitated so long that Coop feared she would change her mind.

Emotion flickered across her face before she whispered, "Belle."

Hollis paused, seemed like he wanted to press for more, but then nodded. He opened his prayer book, cleared his throat, and started talking.

The words washed over Coop, familiar and strange all at once. He'd heard them before—at Collin's wedding, at Leo's. But these words were for him.

"Marriage is not to be entered into lightly," Hollis continued, "but reverently, deliberately, and in accordance with the purposes for which it was instituted by God."

Coop's throat felt tight. These weren't the words of a business arrangement. He and Belle were making vows.

Suddenly his impulsive decision was real.

His gaze fell on Belle. She was trembling now, despite the shawl wrapped around her shoulders. Her lips were pressed into a thin line.

A fierceness rose in Coop's chest. Something protective.

"Will you love her, comfort her, honor and keep her... as long as ye both shall live?" Hollis's voice cut through Coop's thoughts.

One breath. "I will."

Hollis tipped his head toward Belle. "And will you, Belle, take this man to be your lawfully wedded husband? Will you obey him, and serve him, love, honor, and keep him?"

Belle's voice wobbled. "I—I will."

The words were barely audible, threaded with uncertainty. Coop had the sudden, overwhelming urge to reach out and take her hand. To let her know she wasn't alone anymore.

But then he remembered how she'd flinched away from Jason's touch. Remembered the doctor's quiet words: *"Your body is only trying to protect you from what your brain knows you shouldn't have had to bear."*

She'd never had a choice about who touched her.

Coop kept his hand at his side.

"I now pronounce you man and wife."

Belle's eyes jerked up, her gaze slamming into Coop's. Wide. Startled. Like she hadn't quite believed it would really happen until this moment.

Hollis cleared his throat. "I suppose you want to kiss her now."

Panic flared in Belle's expression.

Coop held her stare, kept his voice steady and calm. "We don't need to do that. I know she's my wife. She knows I'm her husband."

Relief flooded Belle's features. Her shoulders dropped slightly, the rigid tension easing just a fraction.

Coop reached into his pocket, felt the cool metal against his fingers. He pulled out the ring—simple, silver, nothing fancy, but solid—and held it out between them.

"This should be proof for everybody in the company that Belle is my wife."

He extended his hand, palm up, letting the ring rest there. An offering. A choice.

Belle stared at it for a long moment. Then, slowly, she

reached out. Her fingers brushed his palm—just the barest whisper of contact—as she took the ring and slipped it on her finger.

Collin clapped Coop on the shoulder, his grip firm and grounding. The women murmured congratulations.

"Still got work to do tonight," Hollis said gruffly. "Watch needs to be set."

Abigail appeared at the edge of their wagon, waiting for him. Even from this distance, Coop could see the way Hollis's stride changed when he spotted her—purpose and belonging in every step.

The small group dispersed, moving back to their wagons and their evening routines. Within moments, Coop and Belle were left standing alone in the growing darkness, surrounded by the sounds of camp but somehow isolated from it all.

Husband and wife.

What now?

Chapter Four

There'd been a meal of fried fish and biscuits, Belle sitting next to Coop on a crate around the fire. She'd never felt so awkward as conversation from his family seemed to pass over both of their heads while they sat silent.

He'd gone to check on the cattle and left her here while everyone in camp seemed to be wrapping up for the night. What was she supposed to do?

Belle lingered near the fire, watching the other women move with practiced efficiency. Evangeline and Alice and Felicity had a system in place. They worked together to put away clean dishes, bank the fire, tuck children into bed. Every movement purposeful.

Belle didn't know where she fit in that rhythm, so she stood to one side.

Evangeline disappeared into one of the tents, carrying her daughter Sara. The little girl's sleepy voice drifted out for a moment before going quiet.

Belle wrapped her arms around herself inside the shawl.

The evening had grown cold. Above, stars were beginning to appear in the darkening sky.

"Belle."

She spun around.

Maddie approached, Jenny on her hip. She quickly pulled Belle into a one-armed hug. The baby cooed between them.

"Congratulations," Maddie whispered against her ear.

The word felt strange between them. But Maddie didn't know—

Belle stood rigid in the embrace until Maddie pulled back.

"Is there anything you need?" Maddie asked, voice probing.

Belle shook her head.

"Will you—be all right?"

What did Maddie mean by the hesitating words?

And then it hit Belle with the force of a physical blow.

She wasn't sleeping in Maddie's wagon tonight, tucked between two crates, buried beneath a blanket so no one could find her.

The thought hadn't fully formed before now. Or perhaps she hadn't allowed herself to think about what it would mean to be married to Coop. Separated from Maddie and the boys and Jenny. It would be noticed in camp if she slept somewhere apart from her husband. People would talk.

Coop had been bedding down with the cowboys at their camp beyond the circle of wagons. Surely he couldn't expect her to—

She mumbled goodbye in response to Maddie taking her leave. The other woman moved off to her own campsite.

As she watched Maddie disappear, Coop approached from the dark between two wagons. He glanced her way as he moved to Alice's wagon to put away a... coffee tin? His movements were casual and unhurried.

"Goodnight," he called over his shoulder to someone out of Belle's sight.

And then Belle and Coop were alone in the growing darkness.

The fire crackled. Somewhere a horse stamped and snorted. Normal sounds. But Belle's heart was racing so fast she could feel it in her throat.

"If you're ready to turn in," Coop said quietly, "the tent's just there."

"What tent?" She barely breathed the words.

He gestured toward the tent beside Evangeline's, in the center of the wagon circle. In the middle of all these folks.

Coop pushed his hat back, rubbed the back of his neck.

At the ceremony, he'd been so certain, so steady while Belle felt like the world was dissolving beneath her feet. But now this moment of hesitation, and somehow that was worse.

"It'll be safer than sleeping out with the cows," he said. "Out in the open."

Belle's mouth went dry. She twisted her hands together. "I didn't know you had a tent."

"I bought it today."

He'd bought a tent today. For her? Where had he got the money?

Belle's gaze flicked to the tent again. It was tucked closest to the center of the wagon circle, more protected than the other one. The safest place, if danger came from outside the circled wagons.

She forced herself to move toward it. This was what she'd agreed to. Her legs felt wooden, disconnected from the rest of her body. She was aware of Coop following close behind, his presence a physical weight at her back.

She ducked through the canvas flap quickly, needing space between them.

But there was no space to be had. Everything inside the tent was close.

And with Coop kneeling at the entrance behind her, there was nowhere to go. Nowhere to run.

Belle's hand gripped the knife in her pocket, tight enough that her knuckles ached.

Get out. The words were right there, trapped in her throat. He'd said this was going to be a business arrangement. Said they wouldn't consummate it. But she couldn't trust that promise. Wanted him gone.

Coop pulled the tent flap closed behind him.

Darkness swallowed them. Just the faint flicker of firelight from outside, yards away, casting barely enough glow through the canvas to make out shapes and shadows.

He took off his hat. Set it aside. Then his boots, unlacing them with slow, deliberate movements.

She knelt on one of two bedrolls, laid out parallel. He didn't seem to notice that she was frozen as he stretched out in the one closest to the door, putting himself between her and the entrance. Between her and escape.

Or between her and danger.

He lay on his back, one bent elbow behind his head. Completely unruffled.

Belle couldn't seem to move from where she huddled at the back of the tent, her whole body coiled tight as a spring.

"I didn't think about you needing a nightdress," Coop said, his voice conversational. "Or other things. You'll have to give me a list of what you'll be wanting or needing."

The thoughtfulness caught her off guard.

He'd made a show of every movement being slow and steady. She could see exactly where his hands were the whole time—one behind his head, one resting on his stomach.

She still couldn't trust that he wouldn't touch her. But the tightness in her chest eased by a fraction.

She remembered the cave. They'd been trapped together in darkness there, absolute and suffocating. He could have done anything he wanted to her then. No one would have ever found out. They'd escaped by crawling through tunnels. The folks from the wagon train hadn't been able to find them.

And he hadn't touched her, other than to keep warm.

"I don't need a nightdress." Her voice came out thin. "I can sleep in this dress."

Coop made a small noise of disagreement. Then: "What kind of house do you want once we get to Oregon? Something made out of logs? Or maybe stone?"

The question was so unexpected that Belle almost smiled.

"My sister wants a big kitchen," he continued when she didn't answer. "She loves feeding everybody."

He was trying to make conversation to put her at ease. That wasn't a requirement of their arrangement.

"I haven't even thought about it," Belle said.

A hint of teasing crept into his voice. "Well, you'd better start thinking. The journey's end will be here before you know it. You'll have to pick out a homestead. Something with water for your cows. A spring or a creek. Place to plant a garden."

The words might have filled someone else with anticipation.

Instead, overwhelming panic crashed over Belle.

A house. Land. Cattle. A garden.

She didn't know what to do in a kitchen. Could barely remember her mother cooking when she was very small, standing at her mother's knee, watching hands knead dough, feeling flour dust settle on her nose. Hands sewing... a dress? A shirt? Those memories were so far away.

She couldn't remember what her mother's face looked like.

How was she supposed to build a life when she didn't know how to live?

Coop's head turned toward her in the darkness. He couldn't possibly see her any better than she could see him—just shapes in the dark—but she felt his gaze.

"I expect you might be more fanciful than Alice," he said, a hint of a smile in his voice. "She's as practical as they come. But if you want two or three windows and fine curtains to cover them and a rug for the floor, we'll make all of it happen."

For one brief moment, Belle could almost see it. A house with windows. Real glass panes. Curtains. A rug on the floor so her feet wouldn't be cold in the mornings. A kitchen where she could learn to cook. A garden where things would grow.

A home.

The desire for it was so visceral it hurt. A physical ache in her chest that made it hard to breathe.

"You don't know me at all," she whispered.

"No," Coop agreed. "But I'd like to."

A pause. Then: "Though I'm not sure you know yourself either, being trapped where you were."

The words hit too close to the locked-away places Belle didn't let herself think about.

She needed to change the subject. "You said you'd teach me how to shoot the revolver."

Coop nodded in the darkness. She could just make out the movement. "I can teach you to shoot a rifle, too."

A rifle. That would be more useful for hunting, wouldn't it? For protecting herself and whatever home she built.

Belle swallowed. "All right."

And somehow—impossibly—a wave of happiness emanated from him. Which had to be her imagination. Had to be fanciful thinking, like he'd said.

Coop turned his head away, settled deeper into his bedroll. His breathing began to even out, slow and steady.

Belle still couldn't make herself lie down.

The air grew cool. She could see her breath in small clouds when the firelight caught it right.

Eventually, her muscles unlocked enough that she could move. She stretched out in her bedroll, but not all the way in. She didn't want to be tangled up in blankets if something happened and she needed to run.

She pulled the knife out of her pocket and tucked it under the thin pillow.

Her eyes stayed wide open, staring into the darkness.

She couldn't trust herself to fall asleep.

Outside, the fire popped and crackled. Someone coughed—one of the night watchmen. Probably. A cow lowed in the distance. Normal sounds of camp settling for the night.

Belle lay rigid, every muscle tense, the knife cold and solid beneath her head.

This was her path forward. Half the cattle. A homestead. Windows and curtains and a garden.

Freedom.

She just had to survive long enough to claim it.

The smell of acrid smoke filled Coop's nostrils.

The taste of it coated his tongue and throat. Heat licked his skin, and somewhere in the distance—screams. The grinding crash of timber giving way. Oliver's voice calling out—

Coop jerked awake.

His eyes snapped open to darkness. Canvas above him. The scent of smoke faded, replaced by damp earth and cold air. It had been a dream. Just a dream.

He lay still, forcing his breathing to slow. Trying to erase memories of the explosion. Forced his racing heart to settle. The nightmare clung like cobwebs. He could still hear Tann's voice echoing in his mind.

Gradually, it faded, and awareness returned.

The tent. The wagon train. Belle. His new wife.

Coop's gaze shifted without moving his head. There—curled into a tight ball at the far edge of her bedroll. As far from him as she could possibly get in the small space.

Her expression was stormy. Even in the pre-dawn dimness, he could make out the worry line between her eyebrows and tension in her jaw.

She was afraid even in sleep.

That growing fierce protectiveness surged through Coop's chest. He'd given her his word: half the cattle, a fresh start, freedom. He'd prove to her that he could be trusted. That he could be the kind of man who kept his promises.

And maybe she'd change her mind about the agreement. Change her mind about him.

He just had to figure out how to keep her alive long enough to get there, because Sarge was still on the loose.

Belle stirred when he slipped out of the tent, her breathing changing rhythm. But she didn't wake.

Coop grabbed his boots on the way out, carrying them so the sound wouldn't disturb her. Outside the tent, the air was sharp and cold, the sky just beginning to lighten at the eastern horizon. Only a handful of people stirred in camp—someone banking a fire, a figure moving between wagons.

Coop sat on a crate and pulled on his boots.

Time to settle things with Leo.

The thought sat heavy in his gut. His brother hadn't cared enough to attend Coop's wedding, but an idea had sprung into Coop's mind last night as he'd done his level best to calm Belle enough for her to sleep. But Coop's idea meant he needed Leo's help.

Leo rode into view just as the sun began to paint the sky pink, coming off watch. Leo dismounted outside the circle of wagons and bent to run one hand down the horse's legs. He didn't glance up at Coop's approach, even though he must've heard Coop's boots crunching in the frost-covered grass.

Coop swallowed back the fury rising at the back of his throat.

He worked to keep his voice level, "I want to make things right between us."

Leo didn't respond immediately. Then, "That doesn't sound like an apology." Leo's voice was flat.

Coop should have known his brother wasn't going to make this easy.

He gritted his teeth. "I've got a wife to take care of now. I'll need the family behind me. Alice stood up with me. And Collin did."

Leo still didn't look up.

Coop felt his hold on his temper starting to loosen.

"And I need to know," he said, each word deliberate, "if you really intend for those cattle to be for the family when we reach Oregon. Or if you mean to keep them all for yourself."

Leo finally turned to face Coop. His hands went to his hips. Even in the dim light, Coop could see the anger in the set of his brother's shoulders.

"Thanks for letting me know what this is really about." Leo's voice carried an edge sharp enough to cut. "Not about making things right. You just want to know if I'm going to give you your share of the cattle."

The accusation stung, made Coop want to defend himself.

But he thought of Belle sleeping in that tent. Thought of the worry line between her eyebrows, the way she'd curled into herself. That knife he guessed she'd tucked under her pillow.

He breathed hard through his nose.

"I've helped wrangle those cattle across the plains and mountains. Put my neck at risk for them more than once." He kept his voice steady with effort. "I think it's only fair that I receive my share when we reach Oregon."

Leo looked him up and down, fire in his expression. Something else, too. Something Coop almost recognized but couldn't quite name.

"I need to know," Coop pushed, "if I'm going to have to start all over when we reach Oregon in a few days."

Leo's jaw worked. It was clear he didn't want to say yes.

"If you follow every rule and every order that I set out for you from now until we cross into Oregon—" Leo's voice was hard, uncompromising. "—I will give you your cattle. But you have to prove to me that you won't squander this inheritance when we get there."

The words made Coop's blood boil. Like Leo was the only one who knew right from wrong. The only one who could make good decisions. Like Coop was still a child who needed managing.

But then Belle's face flashed through his mind again.

Coop had pretended to fall asleep last night, wanting to see how long it would take for her to trust him enough to relax enough to lie down. He must have accidentally fallen asleep before she did, because when he'd jerked awake from the nightmare, she was curled in her bedroll.

How long had she stayed awake? Hours, probably. She deserved a better hand than the one life had dealt her.

"It's a deal," Coop said quietly.

Leo studied Coop's face like he was searching for a lie. Then, "How are you going to keep her alive until you get to Oregon?"

Coop wasn't going to squander this moment. He'd had an idea last night while lying awake, listening to Belle's breathing. It was risky. Unconventional. Exactly the kind of plan Leo would normally dismiss as reckless.

But Coop laid it out anyway. Reminded Leo how Stella had dressed as a man when she and her sisters first joined the wagon train. How she'd fooled everyone for weeks. How Sarge would be watching the wagons, watching the women in camp. He'd never expect Belle to be riding out with the cowboys.

"It gives you and the others time to find him," Coop finished. "To grab him before he can get to her."

He'd halfway expected Leo to tell him it was stupid and to dismiss it out of hand.

Instead, Leo watched him with that considering gaze for a long moment. Then he nodded.

Just once. A single, sharp dip of his chin.

It might be all the approval Coop was going to get. But it was something.

"Thank you." Coop turned and headed back toward camp, his boots crunching on frost-stiffened grass. The sun was coming up properly now, painting the sky in shades of gold and pink. Smoke rose from morning fires as families began to stir.

He stopped by Collin and Stella's tent, where his brother was already awake and moving around outside.

"Need a favor," Coop said quietly.

Collin raised an eyebrow but didn't ask questions. Just listened as Coop explained, then nodded and disappeared into the tent. He emerged moments later with a bundle of clothes and Stella's old hat.

"Good luck." Collin pressed the bundle into Coop's hands.

Coop made his way back to Belle's tent and ducked under the canvas flap.

Belle woke instantly.

She jerked upright, eyes wide and wild, hand going automatically beneath the pillow. Coop saw the flash of metal before she seemed to register where she was. Who he was.

For a moment, she just stared at him, breathing hard.

Their first morning together as husband and wife.

The awkwardness of it settled over Coop like a blanket.

"Morning," he tried, his voice coming out rougher than he'd intended.

Belle's hand came out from beneath the pillow. Empty. Her gaze tracked his movements as he settled just inside the tent entrance.

She looked like a cornered animal. Ready to bolt or fight at the slightest provocation.

It was going to take a long time to build trust between them.

And they only had—what? Ten days? Two weeks at most until they reached Oregon?

Coop wasn't sure that would be enough time. But he'd do everything he could to prove to her that he was worth trusting.

"Alice will have breakfast soon," he said, grasping for something to say that wouldn't spook her.

Belle's expression flickered. "Do you expect me to be helping her? I don't know how to cook."

"I don't expect you to do anything." He paused. "But if

you want to learn how to cook, there's no better teacher than Alice."

He set the bundle of clothes down between them. Belle's brows creased, confusion crossing her features.

"When Collin's wife, Stella, first came to the wagon train," Coop began, "she and her sisters were alone and on the run from some awful men. So Stella dressed like a man and fooled everybody in the company for weeks."

Belle's gaze flicked to the bundle and back to his face.

"The idea is for you to dress like a young man," he said, laying it out carefully, "and ride out with the cowboys. Sarge is going to be expecting you to be in one of the wagons or in camp. That's where he'll be looking. He'll never expect you to be out with the cowboys."

Belle's expression changed to a mix of intrigue and then hesitation. "I can't ride."

"I can teach you. It'll give Leo and the others a chance to find him," Coop continued. "To grab him before he can do something to you. You'll be hiding in plain sight. Surrounded by armed men who know how to shoot."

He could see her wrestling with the idea.

"Half those cattle are going to be yours," he said. "You'll need to know how to ride. How to work with them. This is part of building that life you want."

Belle's gaze lifted to meet his. A sharp determination flickered in her eyes.

"All right," she whispered. "I'll do it."

Coop felt a surge of pride. His wife was terrified. But she was brave enough to face it anyway.

Chapter Five

Belle almost disappeared in the men's clothing.

Coop walked beside her toward where the horses were picketed, the morning sun just beginning to warm the frost-stiffened grass beneath their boots. He stole glances when he thought she wouldn't notice—Stella's old trousers and shirt hanging loose on Belle's slighter frame, the fabric bunching at her waist where he'd helped her cinch a belt tight enough to keep everything in place. She wore Stella's slicker, and Stella's hat pulled low over her braided hair. She could pass for a gangly teenage boy.

As long as no one looked too closely at her face. At those eyes.

She glanced over, caught him staring.

Heat crept up Coop's neck. He jerked his gaze away, fixed it firmly on the horses ahead. The last thing he wanted was to make her uncomfortable. To make her think he was looking at her the way—

He cleared his throat. Shoved the thought away.

They'd walked well outside the circle of wagons now, out toward where the cowboys kept their mounts hobbled in the tall grass. The cattle grazed beyond in a shifting sea of brown and white, their lowing carrying on the cool morning air. From up in the hills, all Sarge would see was livestock and the occasional figure moving among them. If he was watching. And Coop had to assume he was.

Belle's gaze swept the open ground, the distant tree line, the ridges beyond. Coop saw the tension return to her shoulders. The wariness in how she held herself—like she was ready to bolt at the first sign of danger.

"Sarge would have to expose himself to get to us out here," Coop said quietly, keeping his tone matter-of-fact. "We're safe. Surrounded by the herd and armed men. Cowboys are always watching for predators—wolves, mountain lions, rustlers. He'd be spotted before he got within rifle range."

Belle's shoulders dropped just a fraction. The rigid line of her spine eased.

Coop filed it away as a small victory. She trusted his assessment enough to relax. That was something.

They reached the horses. Coop had picked Daisy specifically for Belle—the gentlest mare in the Spencer string, a dappled gray they'd bought in Independence. She was getting on in years, her muzzle gone white, but she was steady and patient. Perfect for someone who'd never been in a saddle.

"This here's Daisy," Coop said, running his hand along the mare's warm neck. Her coat was smooth beneath his palm, the muscle solid. "She's gentle. Real steady. Won't give you any trouble."

Belle looked up at the horse. Her eyes went wide, and despite the bulky men's clothes, she seemed to make herself smaller. Like she could disappear if she just held still enough.

"Have you ever ridden before?" Coop asked. He kept his voice gentle, the same tone he'd use approaching a skittish colt.

Belle shook her head.

"Horses are smart," he said, moving his hand in slow strokes down Daisy's neck. "Smarter than most folks give them credit for. They pick up on how you're feeling—if you're scared or angry or calm." He ran his palm all the way down to the mare's shoulder. Daisy leaned into the touch, huffing out a contented breath that stirred the dust at her hooves. "See? She's telling me she trusts me. That's what this is about. Building trust between you and her."

Belle stood beside him without flinching away, watching his hand move along the horse's neck. Not looking directly at him, but not retreating either.

A beat of hope stirred in Coop's chest. Maybe she was starting to see him as something other than a threat.

"She likes you," Belle said softly.

"Yeah, well." Coop moved to the saddle. "We've spent a lot of time together."

He rested his hand on the saddle's worn leather. "This is where you'll sit. See this part here? That's called the pommel. You can hold onto it if you need to steady yourself, especially when the horse is moving."

Belle reached out tentatively. Her fingers brushed the leather, light as a butterfly landing on a flower. The mare didn't even twitch an ear.

"Subtle movements are always better with horses," he continued, warming to the teaching now that he had something safe to talk about. "They respond to the slightest shift in your weight, the smallest pressure from your legs or the reins. You don't need to pull hard or kick to get them to do what you want. Just a gentle nudge is usually enough."

Belle nodded, her hand still resting on the saddle. She was soaking up every word like she was memorizing it. Like this information might save her life.

Which, out here in the wilderness, with a madman hunting her, it very well might.

"Don't let this mare fool you," Coop said, allowing a hint of warmth into his voice. "She might look big and intimidating, but she's as gentle as they come. You couldn't ask for a better first mount."

Coop brought his attention back to the task at hand. "Now, let's get you up into the saddle. I'm going to need to give you a boost, all right? And after you're up, I'll probably need to adjust these stirrups to fit your legs. That means I might have to touch your feet and legs to get the length right." He paused, made sure she was looking at him. Made sure she heard him. "Is that all right with you?"

Belle's eyes widened. Surprise flickered across her features—genuine surprise—before she nodded. "That's fine."

The fact that she was surprised he'd asked landed heavy in Coop's gut, like a stone. Had every man she'd known not asked permission for something as simple as help mounting a horse? Did every man take what they wanted without asking?

His jaw clenched. He forced it to relax.

"All right." He bent his knee, braced his hands on his

thigh to make a stable step. "Put your left boot here on my leg and push up so you can get into the saddle. Grab the pommel with your left hand, the cantle with your right, and swing your right leg over when you push up. I'll steady you."

Belle positioned her boot where he'd indicated. Her weight settled onto his thigh—light, barely any pressure at all. She was too thin.

She gripped the pommel, took a breath, and boosted herself toward the saddle.

Halfway through the motion, she wobbled. Lost her balance.

Coop's hand shot out on instinct, catching her at the waist before she could fall. "Easy there."

The moment his palm made contact, he felt her go rigid. Just for a heartbeat. That split second of pure fear before she seemed to remember where she was. Who he was.

Finally, Belle settled into the saddle, finding her seat. Daisy stood steady beneath her. Coop made a mental note to give the old girl an apple tonight if he could sweet-talk one out of Evangeline's supplies.

He handed the reins up to Belle. "Hold these light in your hands—not too tight. You're just guiding her, not fighting her. A gentle tug left or right tells her which way you want to go. Pull back gently to stop. That's really all there is to it for now."

Belle's fingers closed around the leather reins. Her knuckles went white with her grip.

"Breathe," Coop said softly. "Remember, she can feel what you're feeling. If you're tense, she'll get tense."

Belle took a visible breath. Let it out slow. Her grip loosened just a fraction.

Better.

Coop knelt in the grass beside Daisy and reached for the stirrups. Tried not to think about how close he was to Belle's leg. Tried to keep his movements professional. Brotherly. Like he'd promised.

He wasn't sure he was succeeding. His hands felt clumsy as he adjusted the leather straps, checking the length against her boot, making sure they'd be comfortable for riding. His fingers brushed her ankle through the fabric of the borrowed trousers, and he heard her breath catch.

"Almost done," he said, keeping his eyes on his work. Not looking up at her. "There. That should do it."

He stood quickly, stepped back. Put proper distance between them. His hands felt too warm, like he'd been holding them too close to a fire.

"Now try walking her," he said, his voice coming out rougher than he'd intended. He cleared his throat. "Just give a slight nudge with your heels. Daisy'll do the rest."

Belle hesitated. He could see the fear warring with determination on her face. Then she pressed her heels gently into the mare's sides.

Daisy started forward at an easy, ambling walk.

Coop watched Belle's face, saw the flicker of panic cross her features as the horse moved beneath her, followed almost immediately by focus. Concentration. Her hands adjusted on the reins, finding the right pressure. Her body shifted slightly, unconsciously finding balance in the saddle.

She was doing it. Actually doing it.

Pride swelled in Coop's chest—warm and fierce and unexpected.

"Good," he said, unable to keep the satisfaction out of his

voice. "Real good. Now try turning her. Use the reins like this..."

Belle gave the reins a gentle tug, as he'd instructed.

Daisy turned left smoothly, responsive to the lightest touch.

"Perfect." Coop nodded his approval. "Now try the other direction."

Belle turned the mare right. Then left again. Getting more confident with each successful turn.

"If she starts to trot—which she probably won't—but if she does, try to rise up a little in the saddle with the rhythm of her movement. Helps you not bounce around so much." He demonstrated the motion with his hands. "Up, down, up, down, matching the horse's stride. But like I said, Daisy's more likely to stop and eat grass than break into a trot."

He went through the rest of the basics. How to stop—gentle tug on the reins, maybe a quiet "whoa." How to back up, though he doubted Belle would need that skill just yet. What to do if the horse got spooked—stay calm, keep your seat, don't yank on the reins or you'll just make things worse.

Though he doubted Daisy would spook at anything short of a lightning strike hitting right next to her. The old mare had seen too many years to be bothered by much.

Satisfied that Belle had the fundamentals, Coop went to his own mount. Scout was a sturdy bay gelding, younger and more spirited than Daisy. Coop swung up into the saddle with the ease of long practice, settling his weight and gathering the reins in one smooth motion.

He positioned himself nearby—close enough to reach Belle if she needed help, but far enough that it wouldn't look like he was hovering. Or like he was paying special attention to one particular "cowhand."

Belle walked Daisy in a wide, slow circle. Her posture gradually relaxed as she got used to the horse's movement, the rhythm of the walk. Her shoulders dropped. Her white-knuckled grip on the reins eased slightly.

She was getting it. Understanding the partnership between horse and rider.

"You're a natural," Coop called out after watching her make several successful turns without any guidance from him.

Belle looked over, and for the first time since he'd surprised her in the back of Maddie's wagon, he saw something that might have been a smile. Small. Reserved.

But there.

"Thank you." Her voice was soft, barely carrying across the distance between them.

Those two simple words made Coop's chest feel too tight. Made him want to do everything in his power to give her more reasons to smile like that. To look at him without fear shadowing her eyes.

"Once we start pushing the cattle today, we can't make it obvious that you're riding with me," he said.

She nodded.

"Are you ready?" he asked gently. "To join the others?"

Belle's hands tightened on the reins. He saw her throat work as she swallowed hard. Saw the flash of fear in her eyes.

But then she lifted her chin. Squared her shoulders in a way that made her sit taller in the saddle.

"I'm ready."

Belle stood beside Daisy, her hands resting on the saddle.

Coop stood on the other side of his horse, rifling through one of his saddlebags. She was grateful he'd given her this moment—one last breath before they had to face the cowboys and make this real.

The riding lesson was still fresh in her mind. Coop had been patient. Careful. He'd kept his touch impersonal.

She didn't know what to make of him.

A memory flickered. She'd woken briefly this morning to the sound of a low moan from Coop's bedroll. A nightmare. She'd recognized it because she had them too. Only moments later, he'd slipped out of the tent quietly, and she'd been so exhausted that she'd drifted back to sleep.

When she'd woken again, he'd been gone.

Coop caught her attention with a tip of his head, and she joined him as he strolled over to meet three other cowboys.

They were dousing their campfire, rolling up bedrolls, preparing for the day's work. The scent of woodsmoke and coffee hung in the cool morning air. A man in a brown felt hat was laughing at something another had said, the sound carrying across the open ground.

Normal. Easy.

"Hallo, you rascals." Coop's voice pitched low. "This is my wife. Belle, this is Rusty"—he gestured to a man with a graying beard and weathered face—"Matt, and Lucky."

Rusty tipped his hat just before he offered Coop a tin mug with steam rising from it. "Saved you the last bit of coffee."

The other two nodded silent greetings.

The words landed strange in Belle's ears. *My wife.*

Coop didn't seem to register her sudden tension.

Where would a wife stand? A wife in disguise? Belle edged slightly closer to Coop. Close enough that she could smell leather and woodsmoke and another scent that was just him.

Coop turned, held out his mug in offer. Steam still rose from the dark liquid inside.

Belle stared at it.

He'd just been drinking from that cup. His mouth had been on that rim. And now he was offering it to her like it was the most natural thing in the world.

A real wife would drink from the cup. Wouldn't hesitate.

Belle reached out and took the mug. Her fingers brushed Coop's as the cup changed hands, and warmth unfurled in her chest.

She lifted the mug to her lips, aware of the cowboys watching. Aware of Coop's gaze on her.

The coffee was black and bitter. Strong enough to make her nose wrinkle before she could stop the reaction.

Coop raised an eyebrow.

Belle dropped her voice. "I usually take it with a little sugar."

Rusty let out a low chuckle. "Sounds like you don't know your new wife too well, Coop."

But Coop held her stare. His gaze steady. Calm.

A small smile tugged at the corner of his mouth. "There's plenty of time for us to get to know each other."

Belle knew he wasn't telling the truth. Knew they had maybe two weeks left before they reached Oregon. Before the arrangement ended and they went their separate ways.

But the cowboys didn't know that. To them, this looked like a new marriage. Young love. A couple just starting their life together.

"It's all right," Belle heard herself say. She took another sip of the bitter coffee, forced herself not to grimace. "Thank you."

She kept the mug, cradling it in both hands for the warmth.

The cowboys went back to their preparations, the moment passing. But Belle felt keenly aware of everything—the weight of the borrowed clothes on her body, the heat from the coffee seeping into her palms, the solid presence of Coop beside her.

And then her neck prickled.

Someone was watching her.

Belle's gaze swept the small group. Found the younger cowboy, Matt—maybe mid-twenties, with dark hair and a lean build—staring at her with an intensity that made her stomach clench.

Not the way men usually looked at her. Not with desire or possession.

This was different. Sharper. Like he saw something the others didn't.

Belle's hand tightened on the coffee mug.

Coop shifted beside her as the man named Rusty moved toward another group of horses. Her gaze flicked to her husband, and he shook his head slightly. As if he'd known she'd gone tense again, nervous about these cowboys.

He took the cup from her suddenly nerveless fingers. Whispered, "It's going to be all right."

She wished she could believe him.

Leo used his boot to push dirt over the last embers from Alice's cook fire. Smoke curled up into the morning air, mixing with the sounds of the wagon train preparing to move out.

He lifted two crates of supplies and carried them to Evangeline's wagon. Tucked them in where they'd stay secure during the day's journey.

Around him, the camp was in motion. Canvas flapped as families rolled tents. Oxen lowed as they were yoked. Children's voices carried on the cool morning breeze.

Leo could see the cattle beginning their slow drift forward. The cowboys had already started pushing the herd.

His gaze found Coop and Belle automatically. They rode flank together, Belle in men's clothing.

Leo shook his head.

Movement from a nearby wagon caught his attention. Collin backed out of the wagon where he must've just settled Stella. Lily Grayson née Fairfax—Stella's younger sister—emerged right after him, a basin of water in her hands. His brother caught a glimpse of him and walked in his direction, his expression grave. Lily gave Leo a tired nod before heading off, probably to empty the basin.

Tension flared in Leo. He hadn't thought to ask about Stella in awhile. Collin's wife had been severely injured in a gunfight. For several days, Doc hadn't been certain she'd pull through. Doc said the baby was still safe, but Stella needed rest. Lots of it.

Collin could probably use someone to spell him in the night. Leo hadn't had the time, not being on the hunt for

Sarge. At least Lily had been helping. Matt had mentioned his wife barely left Stella's side except to sleep.

Another responsibility he was failing at.

"Is Stella alright?" Leo asked.

"She had a bad night." Collin's expression was tight. "The wound is healing well, but carrying a child while recovering from something like that..." He shook his head. "Doc says she needs to stay off her feet as much as possible. I'm hoping she'll be able to rest in the wagon this morning." He straightened his shoulders. "But I wanted to talk to you about Evangeline."

Leo stiffened. "What do you mean?"

"She's seemed quiet the past few days. Stressed. I'm wondering if there's anything she needs from me or from Alice."

Leo wracked his mind for what his brother might be talking about. "I haven't noticed."

The words sounded defensive even to his own ears.

"You've been caught up with a lot," Collin continued. "Being a captain. With Stella and Rob being injured, Evangeline's taken on more work. I don't want her to suffer because she's helping us."

Tension coiled in Leo's chest. The familiar weight pressing down.

He glanced across camp. Evangeline stood talking to one of the other women. Sara at her side. She looked fine.

But Collin was right. Leo had been so focused on managing the company, on keeping Coop in line, on making sure everyone stayed safe, that he'd barely spoken to his wife in days.

The bugle blew. Time to move out.

"I'll check on her," Leo said.

Collin nodded. Headed toward his own wagon.

Leo checked that Evangeline was all right getting their wagon pulled into the line before he moved to his horse and mounted up.

His horse read his frustration and danced underneath him. He forced his shoulders to relax, calmed the horse with quiet words.

This situation with Sarge couldn't go on. Things needed to end. Coop's choices were causing trouble for everyone. For Evangeline. For his family.

Leo had to do something.

The idea had been forming all morning, since the moments when Coop had been laying out his plan for Belle to dress in men's clothing.

Now it was time to put it into action.

Leo rode up beside Owen. His half-brother was on horseback as Rachel pulled their wagon into line. Leo motioned for Owen to follow him away from the wagon, where Rachel wouldn't hear.

Owen frowned but directed his horse alongside Leo's.

The trail ahead narrowed where it cut through a stand of pine. Leo guided his horse around a wagon rolling past, the wheels creaking over exposed roots and rocks. The ground here was uneven and rocky. The kind of terrain that could snap an axle if drivers weren't careful.

Leo scanned the tree line. Perfect cover for someone watching.

"What's going on?" Owen asked.

"We need to end things with Sarge," Leo said. He kept his voice low. Kept his eyes on the woods. "He's endangering everyone in the wagon train. Coop has his wife dressed like a cowhand." He paused. "What if we help Sarge figure out that she's out there with the cowboys?"

Owen's expression went carefully blank. Then his eyes narrowed. "It'll put your brother in danger. Put Belle in danger."

A family's wagon lumbered between them. Leo pulled his horse to the side, letting it pass. The trail rose ahead, climbing toward the mountains they'd cross today.

"Not if we're careful about it." Leo leaned forward in his saddle as his horse picked its way over a rocky section. "We can use her riding out with the cowboys as a way to draw Sarge out. Without putting anyone from the company in more danger."

Owen shook his head. Guided his own horse around a fallen log half-buried in the trail.

Leo's hands tightened on the reins. "We find the right place. Keep it under wraps until we're ready to show him that she's riding with the cowboys."

Another wagon rolled past. Children's voices drifted from inside the canvas. Leo waited until they were out of earshot.

Owen opened his mouth to argue.

Leo drew in a breath. Made himself say the next part. "I can't stand the thought of Evangeline or Sara being hurt. Is that what you want for Rachel?"

Owen's face darkened. He looked away, toward where his own wagon was joining the line. The wheels jolted over a rut.

When Owen looked back, his jaw was tight. "There has to be a better way to do this."

"If there is, I haven't thought of it." Leo pressed forward. His horse climbed the slight grade, hooves finding purchase on the rocky ground. Ahead, the trail disappeared into the pine forest. "If we're ready for him—if we're waiting instead of being caught off guard—we can capture him without anyone getting hurt. We send scouts ahead. Position sharpshooters where they have a clear shot."

Leo's gaze swept the tree line again. Looking for movement. For anything out of place.

Nothing.

But that didn't mean Sarge wasn't out there. Watching. Waiting.

Owen was quiet. His horse sidestepped a boulder jutting up from the trail.

"Fine," Owen finally said. "But if this goes wrong—"

"It won't."

Owen's look said he didn't believe that. "When do we tell Hollis?"

Leo turned his horse toward the front of the train. "Soon. Today."

Chapter Six

"Good evening, Belle."

Alice's smile was warm as Belle stepped out of the tent.

Belle tugged at the skirt of her new dress, a blue calico sprigged with pink flowers. When she'd gone into the tent to change out of the borrowed disguise, it had been folded neatly on her bedroll. Where had Coop gotten the money for it?

Alice was already at work, her hands moving efficiently as she plucked a grouse. Two more birds lay on the ground beside her.

Belle's stomach turned slightly at the sight. But she put on a brave face. "Can I help?"

She needed to learn, didn't she?

Alice's smile brightened. "Of course. Here, let me show you."

Rob sat on a log near Alice, a book open in his lap. But

his eyes kept drifting away from the pages, landing on Alice with a focus that made Belle uncomfortable.

Belle had spent days in the wilderness with Rob after a group of mercenaries hired by Sarge had separated them from the rest of the wagon train. He and Coop both had guarded her, putting their lives at risk. Rob had gone over a cliff's edge grappling with Sarge, and broken his leg badly. She owed him. But had nothing of value to repay him with.

Days ago, he'd suffered the loss of his wagon and supplies when he'd helped pull August out of a cave. Before the accident, he'd worn fine clothes—tailored trousers, pressed shirts, a coat that probably cost more than most people earned in a year. He'd carried himself with an air of entitlement. Now he wore borrowed trousers that looked like something Coop would wear and a man's shirt that had seen plenty of washings.

She didn't fully understand the change in him. He was besotted with Alice, that much was certain.

Alice handed Belle one of the grouse and began guiding her through the process. "You want to grip the feathers like this." She demonstrated with practiced ease, her fingers firm and sure as she stripped feathers away in smooth pulls. "Start here and work your way down to the legs."

Belle took the bird. Its body was still slightly warm beneath the feathers, the weight of it strange in her hands. She tried to mimic Alice's grip, but the feathers slipped through her fingers.

Felicity approached the fire, carrying a wooden pail of water. She moved with the ease of familiarity around Alice. She set a pot on the coals at the edge to heat the water so they could boil the grouse.

Ben trailed behind her mother, carrying a smaller pail. She set it down, then settled onto the ground cross-legged with a bowl and several potatoes, beginning to peel them.

"We brought water up for washing," Felicity said.

Ben glanced up from her work. "Hello."

"Hello," Belle murmured back.

Felicity's gaze settled on Belle for a moment—not judgmental or curious the way Belle was used to. Just... looking.

It felt strange to be a part of this group. Not in hiding anymore.

Alice had already finished plucking her two birds while Belle still struggled with her first. The feathers always slid away, or broke off halfway, leaving ugly patches.

Footsteps approached. Belle glanced up to see Leo, Evangeline, and little Sara walking through camp.

"Leo," Alice called out. "Do you know where Collin went off to?"

Leo barely paused. His eyes swept past Belle like she wasn't there. "Out with the cattle, I expect."

His voice was flat. Cold. And he didn't look at Belle. Not once.

Evangeline glanced back over her shoulder as she followed her husband, Sara's small hand clasped in hers.

Belle focused back on the grouse in her hands. Tried again to grip the feathers properly.

"Don't mind Leo," Alice said quietly. "He's stubborn as they come. It's not that he doesn't like you. He just gets frustrated with Coop."

Rob and Alice exchanged a look—something passing between them that Belle couldn't quite read.

Belle's fingers slipped again. The feathers tore awkwardly, leaving ragged edges. Her face felt hot.

"If I'm making your family uncomfortable—" she started.

"It's got nothing to do with you," Alice interrupted gently. She reached over and took the half-plucked bird from Belle's hands.

Belle had heard whispers of something that had happened with the Spencer family back east. She'd also heard the quiet conversations about Collin's wife—how Stella had been shot, how she was with child, how worried everyone was. That explained why Collin looked so tired lately. But asking questions felt wrong.

Coop and Collin passed through camp then, carrying a heavy barrel between them. Their muscles strained under the weight, cords standing out in their necks. Coop's gaze swept the area until it landed on Belle.

Something flickered across his face. Relief? As if he'd wanted to know she was safe.

Belle turned away quickly, rinsing her hands in the water basin as Alice stripped the remaining feathers from the bird Belle had ruined.

She didn't want Coop to feel things for her. Didn't want him looking at her like that—like she mattered beyond the business arrangement between them.

Alice took over completely, her movements sure and practiced. "I learned how to do this when I was ten. Helping the cook in the kitchen on the grand estate where I worked." She sent a glance over to Rob. Belle didn't understand it, but Rob winked at Alice. "My mother was a maid, and I was a maid, too, and proud of the work I did."

Alice glanced up, her hands never stilling. "Where were your people from, Belle?"

Belle hesitated. "Missouri."

"Where in Missouri?"

"A little town."

Alice didn't seem to notice her questions making Belle feel uncomfortable. "Do you remember much about it?"

"No."

It wasn't quite true. She had buried all those memories of home as a way to protect herself.

One of them snuck into her thoughts now. A memory of sitting in a child-sized rocking chair. Wood worn smooth with use. Her legs had barely reached the floor. And she'd been holding a baby. The weight of it in her arms, the warmth. The baby's dark hair, its small fist wrapped around her finger. Had she been singing to it?

Whose baby?

The memory faded at the edges. Belle blinked it away.

"Where ya been since Missouri?" Ben's voice cut through Belle's thoughts. The girl looked up from where she'd been peeling potatoes. "How come ya can't remember?"

The question hung in the air.

Felicity's head came up sharply. She reached over to touch Ben's shoulder.

Belle glanced to Alice for help. Surely she wasn't supposed to tell the girl her whereabouts.

Alice's hands kept moving as she glanced up with an easy smile. "Some things are harder to remember than others. Especially if they weren't happy times."

Belle dried her hands on a cloth.

Ben stood up suddenly, the peeled potatoes tumbling from her skirt to the ground. "Oh!"

"Ben!" Felicity exclaimed.

But Ben was already running across camp, shouting to the two boys huddled over something Belle couldn't see. "Are those the puppies?" She turned only long enough to shout over her shoulder, "Come see!"

Alice's face brightened. She set down the plucked bird and stood, wiping her hands on her apron. "Puppies? Whose dog had pups?"

"The Martins', I think," Felicity said from where she was picking up the potatoes Ben had left to roll over the ground.

Alice reached down and caught Belle's hand, tugging her to her feet. "Come on."

Belle resisted. "But—"

"When there are puppies to be held," Alice said, "work can wait."

Belle found herself being drawn to where Ben, Alex, and Paul crouched in a circle near the Martins' wagon.

Three tiny puppies squirmed in a blanket-lined crate. Their eyes were barely open, their movements uncoordinated and clumsy. One of them let out a high-pitched yip.

Belle caught movement and glanced up to see Coop, yards away, hauling a different, smaller barrel on his shoulder. The muscles of his arms played as he balanced it precariously. She could hear his faint whistle. When he caught sight of her, a smile stretched across his lips.

"Look, Belle!" Ben's voice brought her back to the present.

Before Belle could step back, Alice was pressing one of

the puppies into her hands. She didn't truly mean to take it, but she couldn't drop it.

It was wriggly and impossibly soft, with a black nose and brown and white fur like down against her palms, warm and silky. It squirmed against her stomach, let out a tiny sound, and something cracked open in Belle's chest.

Joy.

Pure and unexpected.

So unexpected that she instinctively closed it off. Wiped the smile from her lips.

Her stomach knotted, and she quickly handed the puppy back to Alice. "I should—"

She turned and rushed away, passed by Felicity and the fire and the potatoes to duck into her tent, where she pressed her hands against her cheeks. She could still hear the children's excited voices outside. Alice's more calm voice. Ben giggling and then a shriek. "He licked my cheek!"

Belle pressed her eyes closed.

Joy like that wasn't for her. It was too much to hope for.

Think of the cattle. Of a log cabin and that locked door.

That was what Belle needed to focus on. Her future. Not a moment of happiness that was fleeting and soon gone.

But she could still feel the phantom sensation of that soft fur against her palms.

Maybe someday.

Coop jerked awake, his heart slamming against his ribs.

The nightmare clung to him—images of fire and smoke

and the grinding crash of stone giving way. Oliver's voice calling out. Then silence. Terrible, awful silence.

He dragged in a breath. Another. Tried to slow his racing pulse.

The tent was dark around him, the canvas walls barely visible in the faint light that filtered through from the banked campfire outside. Cold air pressed against his sweat-dampened skin, raising goosebumps along his arms.

Then he realized he couldn't hear Belle breathing.

The space beside him—well, not beside him, but at the far back of the tent where she'd positioned herself as far from him as physically possible—was too quiet. That absolute stillness that came when someone was holding their breath.

Coop sat up slowly, careful not to make any sudden movements. "Belle? What's the matter?"

A pause. Tense. Heavy.

He draped one arm over his bent knee.

Then her voice came out of the darkness, sharper than he'd expected. "What's the matter with you?"

The question caught him off guard. "What do you mean?"

"You were making noise. In your sleep."

"What kind of noise?"

"Mumbling. Sad sounds."

Heat crept up Coop's neck. He was grateful for the darkness, grateful she couldn't see his face flush. He rubbed one hand down his face anyway. "I must have been having a nightmare."

He started to shift his weight, intending to lie back down. But he heard her move—the rustle of fabric, the slight scrape of boot against canvas—and he could tell she'd pressed herself even farther back. If she moved any more, she'd be crawling out beneath the tent wall on the other side.

His chest tightened.

She had that knife in her hand. He knew it. Ready to defend herself against him even though he'd never—

Coop swallowed hard, tried to push down the emotions churning in his gut. The terror from the nightmare. The shame. The bone-deep loneliness of lying feet from his wife and knowing she was terrified of him.

"It's not what you think," he said.

Then, before he could stop himself, before he could think better of it, the story started spilling out.

"I worked in a factory back in New Jersey. A powder mill." His hands fisted in his blanket. "I had friends there. Good friends."

He had to close his eyes for a moment against the wave of pain. Oliver's face. Tann's laugh. The way they'd all talked about saving up money, about the lives they were going to build.

"There was an explosion." Coop's throat felt tight. "It was my fault."

The words hung in the air between them.

"I didn't mean for it to happen," he added quickly, the explanation rushing out. "I never meant—"

He stopped. Drew in a breath. Started again.

"We were supposed to work the night shift. Me and my two friends. But we'd been drinking beforehand." Shame burned through him, hot and bitter. "My older brother Leo, he's a stickler for following the rules. He would never touch a drop of alcohol before working. Never. But I'd done it before

—just a bit of a drink to take the edge off the boredom, you know? Thought I could handle it."

Coop heard Belle shift slightly. Not backing away this time. Maybe listening?

He plowed ahead before he could lose his nerve.

"You saw me at my lowest," he said. "When you pulled me out of that creek. That's as bad as I ever got. But I haven't touched a bottle since then. Not one drop."

Silence from Belle's corner of the tent.

Coop wished he could see her face. Wished he knew what she was thinking. Whether she believed him.

"That night at the powder mill," he continued, his voice dropping lower, "I knew I'd gone too far. Had too much. And if I tried working with the black powder and the other supplies we used, I was going to put folks in danger. I told my friends we shouldn't work that night. That we should just not show up."

He could still see the moment. Standing outside the mill in the cold night air. Oliver laughing, saying Coop was being dramatic. Tann saying he really needed the money, couldn't afford to miss a shift.

"One of them said he really needed the wages," Coop said. "And they claimed they hadn't drunk much. I'd been so focused on having my own fun that I didn't know how much whiskey they'd actually consumed."

His hands shook now. He pressed them flat against his thighs to still them.

"So I started for home. To sleep it off." The words tasted like ash in his mouth. "I should have gone to find Leo. Should have told him what was happening, let him handle it. But the last thing I wanted was another lecture about my poor choices and my bad friends and how I was letting the family down."

Coop heard Belle moving again. This time it sounded like—was she lying down?

He kept talking, needing to get it all out now that he'd started.

"I got so sleepy I didn't make it all the way home. Curled up in an abandoned barn at the edge of the mill property." He swallowed hard. "When I woke the next morning, I couldn't believe what had happened."

The images crashed over him. The stone buildings—or what was left of them. Rubble and twisted metal and smoke still rising in the cold morning air. Men shouting. Women screaming. The sick, certain knowledge that his friends would never have survived.

Coop's throat closed up. He couldn't speak for a moment, couldn't push words past the grief that threatened to choke him.

"I was too ashamed to go home at first," he finally managed, his voice barely above a whisper. "Didn't have anyplace else to go, but I couldn't face my family. Not right away. By the time I did go home, Leo and Collin were already making plans. Selling everything to join this wagon train."

He drew in a shaky breath. "We all left New Jersey. But I was the only one running from what I'd done."

Coop lay back down in his bedroll, the movement slow and deliberate so Belle could track it in the darkness. So she'd know he wasn't approaching her.

"I fought with myself for months," he said to the darkness above him. "But I've made a vow now. I'm not going back to the bottle. You can be sure of that. I'm going to be a better man. Make a new life for myself."

The words sounded hollow even to his own ears. How many times had he made that promise before? How many times had he broken it?

But this time felt different. This time he had Belle to protect. Had a reason beyond himself to stay sober.

The silence stretched out. Was she judging him? Did she regret marrying someone with his past? Heat trickled through his cheeks just thinking it.

He lay there in the dark, listening to the distant sounds of camp. Someone coughing. A low murmur of voices from one of the other tents, quickly quieted. The stamp and snort of horses in their picket line.

Then Belle's voice came out of the darkness.

"Your brother counts every mistake you make."

It wasn't a question.

Coop's chest tightened. "Yeah. He does."

A pause. Then: "But that doesn't mean everyone does."

The words landed soft but weighed more than anything else that had been said tonight.

"Some people might just be glad you came back at all."

Coop lay frozen, hardly daring to breathe. The words settled over him with unexpected warmth in the cold darkness.

It was such a simple thing to say. But it ignited something inside Coop's chest. Something that had been locked up tight for so long he'd forgotten it was there.

"I never thought about it that way," he whispered.

He wasn't even sure Belle heard him.

He heard her breathing slow down and even out. The

tension that had been thrumming through the tent began to ease.

She was relaxing. Letting herself drift toward sleep. That felt like a win.

And she'd given him something.

Hope.

Fragile as a soap bubble, but there.

Coop held onto that hope as his own breathing began to slow. As his body relaxed into the bedroll. As exhaustion pulled him back toward sleep.

Maybe he could be more than the sum of his mistakes.

The thought followed him down into slumber—gentler this time, without the nightmares waiting in the dark.

Chapter Seven

The crack of gunfire echoed across the hillside.

Belle flinched as she watched a puff of dust blow up from the hillside thirty yards away.

Coop stood two feet away, arm outstretched with revolver in hand. He lowered it and glanced at her. "Your turn."

She hesitated.

"Come on." Coop gestured for her to join him. "I'll show you how it works."

Belle stepped toward him and let her eyes skitter away from his, focused instead on the rocky outcropping he'd been using for target practice. Two nights had passed since he'd told her about the explosion in the darkness of the tent. Two nights since she'd heard the grief raw in his voice, the shame, the weight of carrying something so heavy for so long.

She hadn't quite known how to act around him since then. Hadn't known what to say or where to look or how to be.

She never would have imagined that a man so confident—so seemingly at ease in his own skin—could carry so much pain. But it had been clear in his voice that night.

And he'd been nothing but kind to her since. Helped her onto the horse each morning with impersonal efficiency, his hands never lingering. Taught her about working with the cattle, patient when she made mistakes. At night around the campfire, she'd watched him endure gentle teasing from his twin brother, Collin, and his sister, Alice. Watched him navigate being part of his family again like a man feeling his way through a dark room.

It made her chest ache in ways she didn't want to examine.

The late afternoon sun slanted across the hillside, casting long shadows. Below them, the cattle grazed in a bunched-up herd, calm and settled for the evening. A handful of other cowboys were on watch farther out, but Coop had brought her here—away from the others, away from where a stray bullet could hurt anyone.

He held out the revolver. Belle took it. The metal was warm from his hand.

"All right." Coop stood beside her, close enough that she could hear him clearly. "You don't need to worry about every single part right now. But there are a few things you really need to know."

He pointed to different pieces of the gun as he spoke. "Keep your fingers clear when you're closing the cylinder—that's where the bullets load. You don't want to get pinched. And be careful when you're cocking the hammer. That's what sets the gun ready to fire."

Belle nodded.

"We don't want to waste too many bullets," Coop continued. "And we don't want to take too many shots and draw attention. But you can definitely take a couple."

The revolver felt unwieldy in her grip. Like it had been made for someone else's hand.

"This gun might be a bit much for you," Coop said, as if reading her thoughts. "There are smaller weapons made to fit a woman's hand better. I could probably procure one for you, if you'd like."

"Maybe I'll get one for myself."

Coop nodded and gestured toward the hillside. "See that outcropping there? With the flat face? That's what I want you to aim for. Nothing but rock behind it for a good stretch, so there's no chance of hitting anything living."

Belle raised the gun. Her arms shook slightly from the weight of it. She thought she was aiming at the rock face, thought she had it lined up, and pulled the trigger before she was really ready.

The explosion of sound made her ears ring.

The recoil slammed through her arms, knocked her back a full step. The bullet kicked up dirt twenty feet in front of her, nowhere near the target.

But it was the sound that got her. That sharp crack echoing across the open ground.

Suddenly Belle wasn't standing on a hillside in the fading evening light. She was back in the brothel. Shouting. A man's voice raised in anger. Then the unmistakable crack of gunfire—once, twice. Someone screaming. The acrid smell of gunpowder mixing with the perfume and whiskey and sweat that always permeated that place.

Rosie. Sweet Rosie with her kind smile. Lying on the

floor with blood spreading across the front of her dress. Dead eyes staring at nothing.

"Belle?"

Coop's voice cut through the memory. Belle blinked hard, dragged herself back to the present. The rocky hillside. The cattle grazing peacefully below. No blood. No Rosie.

"Belle, are you all right?"

"I'm fine." Her voice came out too rough. "It was just—a memory."

Understanding flickered in Coop's eyes. "I'm so sorry."

He took a step closer, near enough that she could see the genuine worry on his face.

"Do you mind if I help?" he asked quietly. "Show you a better way to hold it?"

Belle drew in a breath. Let it out slowly. "All right."

Coop moved to stand beside her, angling himself so he could see what she was doing without getting in her line of fire. "First thing—keep your finger off the trigger until you're actually ready to pull it. Right now, rest it along the side here."

He demonstrated with his own hand, not touching her but showing her where to place her finger against the gun's frame.

Belle adjusted her grip.

"Good. Now your left hand—bring it up to support the barrel. Like this." He showed her with his own hands cupped together. "It'll help with the recoil and give you better control."

She repositioned her left hand. The gun felt steadier already.

Coop stepped slightly in front of her, pointed toward the

rocky outcropping. "When you're aiming, you want to line up these two sights—see them? This one here at the front, and this notch at the back. Get them level with each other and with your target. And keep your arms firm but not locked. Let them absorb some of the kick when the gun fires."

"What am I aiming at?" Belle asked.

"Whatever you want. Pick something on that rock face."

Belle closed one eye, tried to line up the sights the way he'd shown her. There was a dark patch on the stone that might have been a shadow or a stain. She focused on that, took a breath, and pulled the trigger.

The recoil jerked through her arms again, but this time she was braced for it. Didn't stumble back.

The bullet hit wide of her mark—maybe a foot off—but it actually hit the rock face. Chips of stone scattered from the impact point.

"That was good," Coop said. There was approval in his voice but something measured, too. "But you can do better. Don't close your eyes when you pull the trigger."

Belle looked sideways at him. "What?"

A pause. Then he seemed to catch himself. "I mean—keep both eyes open. Trust what you're aiming at."

"I'm more accustomed to men giving me flowery speeches," Belle heard herself say. "Showering me with compliments."

Something shifted in Coop's expression—a flash of understanding.

His gaze held hers. "Is that what you want from me?"

She bit her lip. Looked away. "I'd rather know the truth. So I can be ready to take care of myself."

Silence stretched out. She could feel Coop watching her, could sense him weighing his words.

"So you don't plan to ever be married," he said quietly. "Not really. You won't take a second husband after all this is over."

The question hit a tender place inside Belle's chest. She kept her gaze fixed on the distant hills, the sky beginning to color with the first hints of sunset.

"I have been forced to bow to the whims of others for so long." The words came out rough, honest. "I just want to be on my own."

Belle risked a glance at Coop and found him studying her, thoughtful.

"Do you want to try again?" he asked.

"Show me how to do it correctly."

"I'm going to have to stand close to you."

Belle's heart kicked against her ribs. But she set her jaw, forced her voice steady. "Just do it."

Coop moved behind her. Close enough that Belle could feel the warmth radiating from his body in the cooling evening air. Close enough that she caught the scent of leather and woodsmoke and soap.

He raised his arms, brought them around on either side of her. His arms were longer than hers, and he was able to reach past where her hands gripped the revolver. He didn't grab the gun or take control of it. Just steadied her grip with his palms gently cupping the backs of her hands.

"There," he said, his voice low and calm near her ear. "See how the sights line up now? Front and back level with each other. Your target is right there in the middle."

Belle found she was holding her breath. The heat of him

at her back. The solid strength of his arms bracketing hers. The way his hands steadied hers without gripping, without forcing, without taking over.

Standing this close to a man should have triggered every defense she'd built up over the years.

But it felt—safe. Strange as that was.

"I've got it," Belle whispered.

Coop stepped back immediately. The cool air rushed in where his body heat had been, and Belle felt the loss of it like a physical thing.

She took a breath. Lined up the sights. Picked that same dark spot on the rock face. Kept both eyes open.

And pulled the trigger.

The gun kicked. Her arms absorbed the recoil the way Coop had taught her.

The bullet hit dead center on the dark patch she'd been aiming at. Chips of stone exploded outward from the impact.

Pride swelled in her chest.

"Well done." Coop's voice held genuine pleasure. "That was a fine shot, Belle."

She lowered the gun carefully. Let her arms drop to her sides.

The weight of the revolver felt different now. Less foreign. More like something that belonged in her hand.

"Thank you," she said quietly. "For teaching me."

Coop moved to stand beside her again. "You're a quick learner. Natural, steady hands."

Belle didn't look at him, but standing this close made her realize that something had changed between them. Knowing something from his past, knowing that he was the kind of man who would give her space instead of pushing made her feel... Not friendship, exactly, but safety.

"We should head back," Coop said, glancing at the sky. "Sun'll be down soon. Don't want to worry anyone."

And for the first time since agreeing to this arrangement, Belle felt like maybe—just maybe—she actually could build the life she wanted. Could learn everything she needed to know. Could survive on her own when the time came.

"Hey, Spencer!"

The voice cut across the sound of cattle lowing and men calling to one another. Coop looked up from where he'd been adjusting his saddle, checking the cinch before they pushed the herd for the afternoon stretch.

A man walked toward him—mid-forties, weathered face, wearing a vest despite the heat. Seth. One of the men who worked for Larson.

Coop's stomach clenched.

"He wants to see you," Seth said. Not a question. A summons.

Coop glanced at the cattle, then back at Seth. "We're about to move out. I'm needed here."

"He wants to see you now."

The words landed with the weight of a threat even though Seth's tone stayed casual. Like they were just having a friendly chat.

Coop looked over at Matt. The man had come to the wagon train on false pretenses, fallen in love with Stella's sister Lily. Against all odds, Coop had come to consider Matt a friend over the past weeks. Their eyes met. Matt gave a small nod—he'd keep an eye on Belle while Coop was gone.

"All right." Coop left his horse ground-tied and followed Seth back toward the wagon circle.

With every step, awareness prickled along Coop's spine. He kept his body language casual, hands loose at his sides, but inside he was wound tight as a spring.

Larson stood near his supply wagon, checking something in a leather-bound book. He looked up as Coop approached, and his expression was pleasant enough. Almost friendly.

That made it worse somehow.

"Spencer." Larson closed the ledger, tucked it under his arm. "Walk with me a moment."

They moved outside the circle of wagons. Far enough that their conversation wouldn't carry to curious ears.

"I need you to do a job for me," Larson said.

"What kind of job?"

"There's a man on this wagon train who owes me money. Has for months now. I need you to collect it. Even if you have to use your fists."

Coop's insides coiled tight. "I never agreed to do any kind of job like that for you."

Larson's expression didn't change. "I loaned you money, Coop. Do you have it to pay me back?"

The words hit like a fist to the gut. "No."

"No," Larson echoed. "Because you used that money to buy a tent. And a nice dress for your pretty wife. And that ring—silver, wasn't it? Must have cost a fair bit."

Heat crawled up Coop's neck. Shame and anger warring in his chest.

"If you can't pay me back," Larson continued, his tone

still maddeningly pleasant, "then you work it off. That's how debts get settled out here. I'm sure you understand."

Coop wanted to argue. Wanted to push back. But what could he say? He did owe the money. Had known when he borrowed it that he'd have to find some way to pay it back. He'd just hoped—

He'd hoped he could earn enough by the time they reached Oregon. Hoped he could stand on his own two feet. Prove to Leo that he didn't need his brother's help. That he could take care of his wife without begging for handouts.

But hope didn't pay debts.

Coop walked back toward where the cowboys were mounting up, his stomach churning, his hands numb. The old Coop wasn't gone after all. He was right there, just beneath the surface.

He reached his horse, swung up into the saddle. Around him, the other cowboys were doing the same, calling out to one another, getting ready for the afternoon push. His gaze found Belle automatically. She sat astride Daisy about fifty yards out, talking to Lucky. She was smiling. Not the tight, guarded expression she usually wore, but something more open.

She wasn't running quite so scared anymore.

The thought should have made Coop happy. Instead, it made his chest ache.

The bugle blew. Time to move. He nudged his horse into motion.

The afternoon wore on. The cattle moved at their steady, plodding pace along the trail. The terrain here was mostly flat but cut through with steep drop-offs where the land fell away into rocky ravines. Nothing too dangerous if a body was careful.

Coop's gaze kept returning to Belle.

She rode with increasing confidence now, her posture easy in the saddle. She'd learned to anticipate the cattle's movements, to position herself where she was needed.

A memory flashed through Coop's mind—standing behind her on that hillside, teaching her to shoot. The warmth of her body just inches from his. The clean scent of soap in her hair. The graceful curve of her neck where it disappeared beneath the collar of the borrowed shirt.

He'd wanted so badly to pull her close. To wrap his arms around her and hold her. Not to force anything. Just to hold her.

But he'd known she would hate it. Would feel trapped.

So he'd stepped back. Given her space.

I have been forced to bow to the whims of others for so long. I just want to be on my own.

Her words echoed in his head now. Mixing with the memory of how she'd looked when she hit that rock—the surprise and fierce pride on her face.

She was growing more independent.

Soon she wouldn't need him at all.

Movement caught Coop's eye. Two cattle—a cow and her half-grown calf—had drifted away from the main herd and were heading down a steep incline toward one of the ravines.

Before Coop could call out, Belle had wheeled Daisy around with practiced ease and started down the slope after the strays.

Coop's heart lurched into his throat.

That incline was steeper than it looked. If the horse stumbled, if Belle lost her seat—

He kicked Scout into motion, following her down. "Be careful!"

But she was ahead of him, already guiding the strays back up toward the herd with confident commands and precise positioning. Her horse moved sure-footed over the rocky ground. Belle sat balanced and calm in the saddle, like she'd been doing this for years instead of days.

She glanced back at him as the cattle rejoined the herd, her face lit with exultation.

"I got them!" she called out.

"I saw." Coop's voice came out gravelly. "You did good."

But as the words left his mouth, heaviness settled deeper in his gut.

She wouldn't need him anymore.

Their arrangement would end when they reached Oregon, and Belle would take her half of the cattle and disappear into her new life. The life she wanted—alone, independent, free.

And Coop would be left with the same old problems he'd always had.

He guided Scout back to his position on the far side of the herd, trying to shake off the dark thoughts. Trying to focus on the work.

That's when he felt the weight of a gaze.

Coop looked up.

Leo sat astride his horse on the opposite side of the herd, maybe a hundred yards away. But even at that distance, Coop could read his older brother's expression. The hard set of his jaw.

Leo had been watching him. Had seen—what? Coop chasing after Belle? Coop worrying over her?

Or maybe Leo had seen Seth call Coop away. Maybe he'd noticed Coop's conversation with Larson.

Maybe he already knew about the debt.

Coop looked away first. Couldn't hold his brother's gaze.

He'd been so determined everything was going to be different this time.

But he didn't know how to fix anything.

Chapter Eight

The creek burbled over smooth stones, the sound peaceful in the evening quiet. Coop stood on the bank with a fishing pole in his hands and watched Belle carefully thread a worm onto her hook, nose wrinkled.

They'd stopped a little before sunset—Evangeline and Sara, Collin and Stella, he and Belle. Found this little creek running alongside the trail, its water clear and cold from the mountains. Perfect for trout, if they were lucky. Hollis had declared it safe enough for a little while. Didn't mean Coop wasn't keeping an eye on the woods.

Time was running out. That's what Coop kept thinking as he watched Belle. They were getting closer to Oregon with every mile. How long did they have left? A week, maybe.

He tried to force away the melancholy thoughts and enjoy these moments together.

This adventure had started back at camp. Sara had been begging to go to the creek, and Evangeline clearly wanted to give her daughter a treat. Evangeline had tried to cajole Leo into taking them fishing. But Leo had waved them off with barely a glance, saying he had wagon train business to attend to. Some meeting with Hollis and the scouts.

Collin had offered to take them after a nudge from Stella, who'd been sitting by the fire with Rob and Alice. Lily sat beside her sister, adjusting the pillow behind Stella's back. Matt had just brought fresh wood for the fire before riding out with the cattle. And Coop—seeing an opportunity, feeling desperate—had talked Belle into coming along.

"I'm glad we came," Evangeline said now, smiling at Belle from where she sat on a smooth boulder near the water's edge. Sara was beside her, dropping pebbles one by one in the creek. "It's nice to get away from camp for a bit."

Tension threaded in Evangeline's voice. A tightness beneath the pleasant words. Coop heard it but didn't say anything. Leo wouldn't appreciate Coop butting in. But Evangeline had been jumpy for days. Was someone bothering her?

Collin stood a few feet upstream, casting his line with practiced ease. He grinned at Coop. "You sure you remember how to bait a hook, brother? Or are you going to leave all the fish for me?"

Coop rolled his eyes. "I think I can manage."

He turned to Belle, who was watching Collin with an expression somewhere between curiosity and amusement. "Here, let me show you how to tie it off so the bait doesn't slide down."

Coop moved closer, reached for Belle's hands. Their fingers brushed as he guided her through the knot, and a spark shot up Coop's arm.

He wondered if she felt it too. But her expression stayed unreadable—that careful mask she always wore.

"You are hopeless," Collin called out. "Belle, I can help you if you'd like. I always caught the biggest fish when we were kids."

Belle's mouth curved. Not quite a smile but close. "Is that so?"

"Oh, absolutely." Collin cast his line again with a flourish. "Coop and I used to sneak down to the creek that ran through the Old Man's property. One time we tried to catch a catfish with our bare hands. Coop ended up falling in, and Ma was furious about all the mud he tracked into our tenement."

Belle's eyes narrowed. "That sounds like trouble."

"Always," Collin agreed, grinning at the memory.

The warmth in Collin's voice made Coop's chest ache. Those had been good days. Before he had made a mess of everything.

You got part of the money I wanted, but it's not enough.

Larson's voice echoed in Coop's head. The hushed conversation from this morning when Larson had confronted him as he'd come off watch. Coop had managed to collect half of what the other man owed Larson.

I'll need you again. Soon.

The words sat in Coop's gut like stones.

"Leo taught me how to fish earlier in this journey," Evangeline said, the words pulling Coop back to the present. She glanced at Belle with a gentle expression. "He's almost as patient as Coop. I'm glad you're here with us. It's nice to have another woman around."

Belle looked surprised.

Sara splashed the water with a gleeful noise.

"Do you like to read?" Evangeline asked Belle.

Belle's expression darkened, and she ducked her head. "I never went to school. I can't read or write."

He battled the urge to step in and reassure her, interrupt before Evangeline could say something hurtful.

He needn't have worried.

Evangeline's expression filled with compassion. Her voice was gentle. "I could teach you. I have some books in the wagon. I could lend them to you if you'd like to learn."

Belle turned her head, still not meeting the other woman's eyes. "I'd—I'd like that."

Warmth spread through Coop's chest. Evangeline was offering friendship. Collin had teased like Belle had always been part of their group.

It felt right. Like Belle belonged in their family.

If only it were real.

Collin tugged in his line and moved closer to Coop, lowering his voice so the women wouldn't hear. "Anybody who looks at you can see that you're lovesick over her."

Coop tensed. His hands tightened on his fishing pole. "It's not like that."

Collin raised an eyebrow, his expression skeptical. "Sure it isn't." He clapped Coop on the shoulder. "But I'm happy for you, Coop. You deserve to be happy."

The words twisted like a knife in Coop's gut. He was lying to his brother. To all of them.

Even to Belle.

The debt to Larson. The collections he'd been forced to make. The way he was slowly being dragged back into the exact kind of mess he'd promised her he'd left behind.

I'm not going back to the bottle. You can be sure of that. I'm going to be a better man.

The promise echoed in his mind. But was he? Was he really becoming a better man?

"Check your bait," Coop suggested to Belle, forcing his attention back to the moment. To this small slice of peace.

Belle looked up at him. Their gazes met and held.

For a moment, it felt like the rest of the world faded away, as if it was only the two of them, the sound of the creek, the golden light of the setting sun painting everything warm.

Belle's cheeks lit with a faint blush that made Coop's heart skip a beat.

She looked down quickly, suddenly fascinated by the fishing line in her hands. "I think I've got it now."

She'd never reacted like that before. To anyone. Coop had watched her around the other cowboys, around the men in camp. She was always guarded. Careful. Ready to run or fight.

But just now, for that brief moment, she'd let him see something as it was. Unguarded.

Hope surged in Coop's chest—dangerous and foolish and impossible.

"Ma!" Sara shrieked happily. "Fish!"

Distracted by the girl, it took Coop a moment to realize Belle's line was dancing in the water.

"Oh!" Belle's eyes went wide. "Is that—?"

The tip of the pole bent. She gripped it tighter, unwilling to give up. "Oh! Coop—help!"

It might've been the first time she'd used his name, and he felt his face heat with pleasure as he hurried to her side.

"I'm afraid I'll drop the pole!"

"You won't," he said. He didn't take it from her, but she sent him a frantic glance and tried to move to him. Her foot slipped on the muddy bank, and it was the most natural thing in the world for him to grasp her waist in both hands.

His boot tangled in the hem of her skirt, throwing him off balance. When he regained his footing, her shoulder pressed against his middle. When she didn't flinch or cower away, he felt a momentary flush of triumph.

He had to clear his throat to get words out. "All right?"

Steady on her feet now, she murmured, "Yes."

"Pull him in," he encouraged.

She gave a yank that landed the fish on the bank. It flopped and flipped. Coop let go of her as she eyed it curiously. Sara scampered over. And Coop caught a smirk from his brother.

Belle laughed at Sara's happy exclamation, the sound rusty and clear and beautiful. When Belle looked up at him with unfettered joy shining in her expression, he knew.

This moment—this perfect, golden moment—was everything Coop wanted.

Renewed determination stirred inside him. He didn't know how, but he was going to figure out a way to get free of Larson. Give Belle more moments like this.

Win her heart.

This was a taste of what it could be like. A glimpse of the life he wanted.

It would kill him if his chance for happiness slipped through his fingers.

He couldn't let that happen.

Camp was quiet this morning. Almost peaceful.

Belle stood near the cooking fire, wiping her hands on her apron. She'd helped Alice with breakfast and only partially burned the biscuits this time, which Alice had declared a victory. The company had a rare morning off, and families were taking advantage of it. Washing clothes. Mending harnesses. Resting.

Belle wore her dress today instead of the men's clothing. It felt strange now, being back in skirts. Though she wasn't entirely sure who she was anymore.

She'd gotten used to things in camp. That realization settled over her with something like surprise. Some of the women still looked at her with judgment in their eyes—Mrs. Henderson, a few of the older matrons who whispered when Belle walked past. But most people had stopped staring. Had accepted her presence, or at least tolerated it.

Most of the men left her alone now. Kept their distance. When she wore Stella's disguise, she also wore the gun belt and revolver at her waist.

But there was someone watching her now.

A teenaged boy—maybe fifteen or sixteen—stood across camp near one of the supply wagons, glancing over at her, then looking away quickly when their eyes met. Her skin crawled with awareness.

Belle's hand drifted to the knife at her belt. She was thinking about marching over there and asking him outright what he wanted when movement caught her eye.

Coop.

He strode into camp from the direction of the cattle, his

long legs eating up the distance. His gaze swept the area—checking, always checking—making sure everything was safe. His eyes passed right over the teenage boy without pausing.

But Belle's heart did a strange little skip when Coop's gaze found her.

She was happy to see him.

When had that happened? When had Coop become someone she looked forward to being with?

Somewhere along the trail, without her quite noticing when, Coop had become safe. Someone who kept his word. Who protected without controlling. Who taught without demanding.

Someone who'd never once made her feel like she owed him anything.

Coop carried a bundle in his arms. Cloth wrapped around something that shifted and moved as he walked.

"Morning," he said as he reached her. Then, with that half-smile that made something warm unfurl in Belle's chest: "Will you sit down with me for a few minutes?"

Belle nodded, suddenly unable to find her voice. She moved to the crate Alice had left near the fire and sat down, her hands folded in her lap.

Coop knelt on the ground in front of her.

"I've got a gift for you," Coop said.

Belle's first thought was the derringer he'd mentioned. The small gun that would fit her hand better than his heavy revolver.

But the bundle in his hands moved, wriggling against the cloth.

Belle's breath caught.

Coop carefully unfolded the shirt, and Belle saw the puppy. The same one she'd held the other night—the one that had been so soft and warm in her hands.

"Coop, I can't—" Her voice came out strangled.

But he had already placed the puppy in her hands. A squirming ball of fur, much more awake than it had been that night. Its tiny paws scrambled for purchase. Its pink tongue lolled out.

And then it started licking her chin.

A laugh burst out of Belle before she could stop it.

When she looked up, Coop's gaze was fixed on her face. Like he was memorizing the moment.

Belle's cheeks heated. She dropped her eyes, that odd feeling twisting her insides into knots.

Her fingers played in the puppy's fur. So soft. Impossibly soft. The puppy wriggled and turned, then started chewing on the sleeve of her dress with tiny needle-sharp teeth.

Coop reached over, gently disengaging the little animal. "Easy there. That's not food."

The puppy yawned—a huge yawn that showed all its baby teeth—then settled more calmly in Belle's lap.

Belle's heart drummed in her ears. "I don't even know what to do with a puppy," she heard herself say.

Coop's expression softened. "That's all right. We can learn together. I've never had a dog before either."

"You mean until the end of the trail?"

The words emerged before Belle could think them through. Before she could soften them or take them back.

Coop's smile faltered, and she saw the flash of hurt before his features smoothed and he nodded.

The silence stretched between them, heavy with something Belle couldn't name.

"Our deal wasn't supposed to include any gifts," she said quietly.

"We can be friends." Coop's voice was steady. Certain. "That doesn't depend on the deal."

Friends.

Belle looked down at the puppy in her lap. She knew she should refuse this gift. Knew that gifts always came with strings. With expectations. With prices that would be collected later, when she least expected it.

Men had given her gifts before. Flowers. Ribbons. Pretty words and promises. And they'd all wanted something in return. Always. Every single time.

But she didn't want to think Coop was like those men. She didn't want him to be like them.

And maybe—maybe he wasn't. Maybe gifts from Coop really were just gifts. Maybe friendship with him could be something simple and good and safe.

Still, she should refuse. Should protect herself. Should remember that letting people get close always ended badly.

But the puppy chose that moment to turn itself in a slow circle on her lap, then lay down. It put its head on its tiny paws with a little huff, its eyes already drifting closed.

Belle couldn't resist. Her hand settled on the puppy's back, feeling the rise and fall of its breath. So small. So trusting.

Belle desperately wanted the puppy for her own.

"What will we do with it while we're herding cattle all day?"

Coop's smile returned. "I'm pretty sure I know a little girl I can convince to help watch her for you during the day."

"Ben." The name came easily. Belle had noticed how the girl gravitated toward her.

"She's really taken to you," Coop said.

Belle swallowed hard. "I don't know if that's a good thing."

"It's a good thing." Coop's voice was firm. "It's definitely a good thing."

Belle wanted to believe him. Wanted to believe that people caring about her wouldn't end in disaster. That letting a child get attached wouldn't set them both up for hurt when Belle took her cattle and left.

But she didn't know how to say any of that out loud.

"You should give her a name," Coop said, gesturing to the puppy. "Can't just keep calling her 'the puppy.'"

Belle looked down. The puppy was fast asleep now, its breathing deep and even. "I don't know what to name her."

"How about Daisy? Like the horse?"

Belle shook her head. "That's already taken."

"Scout?"

"That's your horse."

"Fair point." Coop was grinning now, clearly enjoying this. "What about something fancy? Like... Duchess. Or Countess."

Despite herself, Belle felt her mouth curve. "She doesn't look like a Duchess."

"Princess?"

"No."

"Lady?"

"Stop." But Belle was almost smiling. Almost.

Coop held up his hands in surrender. "All right, all right. You don't have to decide now. Take your time. Get to know her. The right name will come."

Belle stroked the puppy's soft fur. Let herself feel the simple pleasure of it. The warmth. The trust.

Maybe this was enough. This moment. This friendship Coop was offering. Maybe she could have it while it lasted, even knowing it would end when they reached Oregon.

Coop stood, brushing dust from his knees. He settled his hat more firmly on his head, like he was preparing to leave.

"Wait." Belle's voice stopped him.

He looked at her, eyebrows raised in question.

"Thank you," Belle said. The words felt inadequate. Too small for what she was feeling. "For the puppy."

She paused, made herself say the rest. "And I never thanked you for ... stepping in. For marrying me when I needed help. I'm glad we can be friends. At least until this is all over."

Until this is all over.

The words hung in the air between them. A reminder. A boundary. A promise that this was temporary.

Coop's hat cast his face in shadow. Belle couldn't see his eyes, couldn't read his expression. There was something enigmatic in the set of his jaw, something she couldn't understand.

The tension between them felt strange. Thick. Like there were words neither of them was willing to say.

"Coop!" A man's voice called out from across camp.

Belle looked over. A man she didn't recognize—one of the supply wagon drivers, maybe—gestured for Coop to come with him.

Coop's jaw tightened. He glanced between Belle and the man, clearly torn.

"You should go," Belle said quietly. "I'll be fine."

Coop hesitated for one more moment. Then he nodded. "Take care of her." He meant the puppy, but the way he said it felt like he meant something more.

Belle watched him walk away, his long strides carrying him quickly across camp. The man fell into step beside him, speaking in low tones Belle couldn't hear.

She looked down at the sleeping puppy in her lap, held that tiny warm body close, and let herself have this moment.

For now, just for now, she could let herself want this.

Could let herself believe it was real.

Chapter Nine

"You need to make sure he pays up."

Larson stood beside his supply wagon, arms crossed over his chest. Evening had settled over camp, fires banked for the night, families tucked into their wagons. The quiet sounds of a wagon train at rest—low voices, the stamp of horses on the picket line, the distant lowing of cattle settling down for the night.

Coop's jaw tightened. "Why does he owe the money now? What's going on?"

Larson's expression didn't change. That pleasant, reasonable look that made Coop's skin crawl. "I can call my loans anytime I want to."

The words landed like a threat. Do what I say, or I'll call in your debt. Before you have any chance of paying it back.

Coop's hands fisted at his sides. "I'll handle it."

The words tasted like ash in his mouth.

He turned and walked away before Larson could say anything else. Before Coop could say something he'd regret.

The camp stretched out around him in the gathering darkness. Most families had already turned in—lantern light glowing through canvas wagon covers, creating pockets of warmth in the cooling night. A baby fussed. A woman sang softly. Normal sounds. Peaceful sounds. Everything Coop wanted and couldn't seem to hold onto.

He wasn't going to threaten some poor man who probably couldn't afford to pay back whatever Larson had loaned him. He'd figure out another way. Had to. He wasn't going to be that person.

He'd find the man tomorrow. Talk to him reasonably. See if they could work something out. Maybe the man could make a partial payment. Maybe Coop could convince Larson to give him more time.

Maybe, maybe, maybe.

Coop was so lost in his thoughts he didn't hear footsteps behind him until Collin's voice cut through the darkness. "It's time to go on watch."

Coop glanced over his shoulder. "I know."

"What are you doing with that guy?"

Coop stopped. Turned. His twin brother stood a few feet away, silhouetted against the glow of a nearby fire. Collin's expression was hard to read in the dim light, but Coop could hear the concern in his voice. And the suspicion.

"It's none of your business." Coop started walking again.

Collin fell into step beside him. "I've heard some whispers about him around camp. Roughing up folks. But nothing substantiated, so Hollis can't get rid of him."

"I said, it's none of your business." Coop's voice came out harder than he'd intended.

"I thought you were trying to be different."

The words hit like a fist to the gut. Coop stopped walking, spun to face his brother. "I am."

"Then why are you sneaking around with a man like that?" Collin's voice was quiet but insistent. "Why are you keeping secrets?"

Coop shook his head. Couldn't explain without revealing everything.

"I thought you wanted to be a better man for Belle," Collin pressed.

And Coop snapped.

"What do you think I'm trying to do?" The words burst out, loud enough that Coop had to check himself, lower his voice. "I'm trying to provide for her. To show her why we should stay together."

The moment the words left his mouth, Coop knew he'd said too much.

"What are you talking about?" Collin's expression shifted. Confusion. Then understanding.

There was no taking it back now. No way his brother was going to let that statement go.

Coop dragged a hand over his face. "Belle and I made a deal. Stay married until the end of the trail, then go our separate ways." He didn't mention the cattle. His brother didn't need to know how deeply Coop had gone into this.

"Why would you do that?"

Because it was the only way I could keep her close. He didn't admit it aloud. The words felt too raw.

"She needed help," he said instead. "Needed safety and a chance for a fresh start. She's a decent person. Hollis was gonna throw her out of the company—"

"So you up and married her?"

He could hear the censure in Collin's voice. An echo of Leo's lectures. *You don't think, do you?*

Collin glanced over his shoulder. "And now you're tangled up with Larson?"

"I'm handling it," Coop growled.

Collin stopped. His crinkled brow viscerally reminded Collin of Pa when Coop had gotten into an argument with a kid in the churchyard. The memory hurt, and Coop shoved it away.

"It doesn't matter how it started." Coop tried to show his seriousness with his voice. "I want things to be real. She matters to me, Collin. She deserves better than what she's been through. I want the best for her."

Collin was quiet for a long moment. "What if wanting the best for her is letting her go?"

The words punched straight through Coop's chest and left him hollow.

"Coop!" Leo's irritated voice called out from the cowboy campfire. "You're on duty!"

"Yeah!" Coop called back, pricking with anger. "Heading out now." He looked at Collin. "I gotta go."

"Coop—" Collin started.

But Coop was already walking away. He reached the horses and rested his head on his fist on the saddle. The nearby creek burbled in the darkness, a reminder of this morning's escapades. The moon was just a sliver tonight.

He'd thought Collin was on his side. That he believed Coop could be different.

Coop felt betrayed, a bitter taste in his throat.

What if wanting the best for her is letting her go?

He'd glimpsed what a life with Belle could be like. Had

seen Belle laugh and relax around his family. Had felt her lean into him when they caught that fish together. Had watched her hold that puppy with so much tenderness.

If his own brother couldn't believe he could be a worthy husband, how could she?

Lively music drifted across the camp in the night air. The moon hung full and bright overhead, casting silver light across the camp. The night was cold but clear—no snow, just that sharp bite in the air that made breath visible. Belle wore the shawl she now suspected Coop had bought for her, wrapped tight around her shoulders.

She sat on a crate near the campfire, her puppy—still unnamed—curled in a basket at her feet. Owen played his fiddle while Rachel swayed gently beside him, Molly sleeping against her shoulder. Ben sat cross-legged on the ground, clapping to the melody.

Alice and Rob had joined them, Rob next to Ben on the ground with his mending leg outstretched in front of him. August and Felicity, too.

The music was different from anything Belle had heard in the saloon. No raucous laughter. No drunken singing. No leering men calling for faster, louder, wilder.

The melody tugged at Belle's memory. A fragment from before the brothel. Before Pa died. A man's voice—her uncle, maybe, or her father—humming while he chopped wood. A smile thrown her way as she'd picked up the pieces and stacked them against the lean-to wall.

The memory hurt. Reminded her of what should've been.

Movement caught Belle's eye. Coop slipped back into camp from the direction of the creek, his silhouette dark against the glow of the firelight.

Something was wrong with his gait. He favored his left side, as he'd done after getting into a fistfight with Rob, before they'd made the fragile peace that characterized their relationship now.

Apprehension swamped Belle's chest. Had there been trouble?

As Coop came to stand behind her, the puppy roused and scrambled out of the basket, tail wagging. Coop squatted down to pet her, his knee bumping Belle's. The little dog licked his hand enthusiastically, and despite her worry, Belle felt her mouth curve slightly.

Ben scrambled to her feet. "Uncle Coop!" The girl grabbed his hand and then Belle's. "Dance with me! Mama and Papa are dancing. You have to dance, too! C'mon, Belle."

Belle glanced over. Sure enough, August had carefully pulled Felicity to her feet. They weren't quite in rhythm with the music, but there was something beautiful in the way they moved together—August's hand steady at his wife's waist, his head tilted to catch the music, a smile on his face Belle had never seen before. Not the strained, angry expression he'd worn for weeks before she and Coop had been lost in the underground cave. This was peace. Felicity's expression was soft with love as she guided him through the simple steps, her hand light on his shoulder, trusting him to lead even as she quietly directed their path.

"C'mon, Belle!" Ben repeated with a tug of her hand.

"I don't think—" Coop started, his voice gentle. "Belle might not want to dance. Not everyone likes dancing."

He was giving her an out. The realization unfurled something both warm and uncertain in Belle's chest.

"I'll dance. With you." The words emerged before Belle could think them through.

Coop's eyes widened with surprise.

"I'll watch the puppy!" Ben scooped up the little dog and settled back onto the ground, looking pleased with herself. "Hey, what're you going to name her?"

Belle shrugged, caught by surprise at how quickly the girl had changed her mind about dancing.

Owen struck up a new tune—still gentle, but with more movement to it. A proper dance.

Coop straightened slowly, extended his hand toward Belle. She stared at it for one breathless moment. Then she accepted it.

When Coop's hand closed around hers, a soft tremor went through her body.

Not fear. No, this was something she'd never felt before.

Over the past four years, everything had been taken without permission. A man's touch had meant violation, pain, powerlessness. But this time, she'd chosen it.

Coop respectfully placed his other hand carefully at her waist and held her like she might break if handled roughly.

She'd danced plenty of times with paying customers, but never like this.

While she and Coop moved together, Belle let herself look at him. Really look. The lines at the corners of his eyes from squinting into the sun while driving cattle all summer.

The square set of his jaw. The careful way he kept distance between their bodies even while dancing.

She'd thought he would be just like all the others. But from the first night, he'd been proving her wrong. He wasn't like anyone she'd known before.

This whole family was different from everyone she'd known before.

The music swelled, and Coop twirled her under his arm. Belle let out a surprised laugh as she spun.

When he caught her waist in his hand again, they were standing closer than they ever had before. Close enough that Belle felt the warmth radiating from his body and saw every detail of his face in the moonlight.

For one suspended moment, neither of them moved.

Then Coop quickly stepped back, returned them to the proper dancing position.

"Spin her again!" Ben called out gleefully.

Belle flushed, only now remembering others were watching.

One corner of Coop's mouth turned up. He whispered, "I forgot about them, too."

He'd known what she was thinking.

She trusted him.

The sudden realization hit her like a physical blow. Made her heart stutter in her chest.

She trusted Coop.

When had that happened? When had this man gone from stranger to protector to—to whatever he was now?

Coop's brows creased.

Had he sensed her sudden uncertainty?

He swept her gently out of the dance, led her to where

Rachel sat near the wagon with the baby sleeping against her shoulder.

"Is everything okay?" Coop asked quietly.

Belle shook her head. Couldn't find words.

"I'll get you some water." Coop squeezed her hand once—she hadn't even realized he was holding it—then moved away to the water barrel sitting near one of the wagons.

Belle sank onto the ground beside Rachel, her legs suddenly unsteady.

"You look like you've just seen a ghost," Rachel said softly. Her expression was kind. Concerned.

"Nothing like that." Belle wrapped her arms around herself, shawl pulled tight. "I think... I might like my husband. Maybe that's a bad choice."

Rachel spoke thoughtfully. "If there's anything I've learned about this family, it's that they are as tight-knit as they come. Good people. Even if Coop has strayed from the flock a bit, he had a good raising."

Belle stared at the fire. Watched the flames dance and flicker.

"My father died when I was fourteen," she heard herself say. The words came slowly. "My uncle... or a family friend? I'm not certain of his relationship to Pa, only that he'd lived nearby ever since I can remember. He was meant to take care of me. He was supposed to—"

Her throat closed. She hadn't spoken about this to anyone. Not ever. She forced the words out anyway.

"He turned me over to a man who owned a saloon. I don't remember—" She shook her head. "He said the man would take care of me. I asked if he would come back. But he just... left me there."

The fire crackled. Somewhere in camp, a child laughed. Across the fire, Ben leaned into Felicity's side, still cuddling the puppy.

Belle caught movement in her peripheral vision. Coop, standing in the shadows behind one of the wagons. He'd come back with the water dipper but must've stopped when he heard her voice. He was waiting there, and she knew he heard every word. Everything inside her said she should stop talking. No one needed to know.

But if she truly considered him a friend, there was no reason to hide this from him.

"Everything was a shock at first," she murmured. "What they—what they expected of me. One of the older girls helped me get dressed."

She watched idly as the puppy climbed out of Ben's lap and took several steps in her direction. It was easier to watch the puppy than to look at Rachel. Or Coop.

Belle's hands clenched in her lap. "I hated the way the clothing felt the moment it touched my skin. Hated how revealing it was. How it made me feel like—like I wasn't even human anymore. Just something to be looked at. Used."

Rachel's hand found Belle's. And again, she didn't flinch away.

The puppy made her way to Belle. She scooped up the pup into her arms, thankful for the warmth of the small body against her sternum.

Belle made herself keep it vague, knowing Ben sat within earshot. "After the first customer, I couldn't stop crying. That same girl who'd helped me get dressed—she came into my room. I thought she would offer comfort. Or help me escape." Belle's laugh was bitter. "She slapped me across the face. Told me tears weren't going to help. Ordered me to go back into the saloon and meet someone else."

The fire popped, sending sparks spiraling into the dark sky.

"That's when I realized no one was coming to help me," Belle said quietly. "I was trapped."

Coop shifted his feet in the shadows. She tucked her chin in the pup's fur, unable to look up.

"I tried to run away." The words kept coming. "Virgil brought me back. He beat me so badly I couldn't walk for two days. Beat all the fight out of me."

Belle lifted her eyes, met Coop's gaze.

His expression was filled with compassion. Pain—not for himself, but for her.

She remembered when he'd told her about the explosion. About losing his friends. About the grief that had driven him to drink.

He couldn't understand exactly what she'd been through, but he understood enough.

"I stopped fighting after that," Belle said. "Went numb. Learned to keep my head down and do what I was told. Until I saw—Sarge kill another girl in cold blood. I knew if I stayed, one day that would be me."

"Belle." Rachel's voice was soft. "I'm so sorry. What they did to you—it was evil."

Belle stared at the fire.

Rachel was quiet for a moment. Then: "There's a verse in the Psalms. It says, 'The Lord is close to the brokenhearted and saves those who are crushed in spirit.'"

Belle's chest tightened. She'd heard the other women in

the wagon train talking about God. But God wouldn't want anything to do with a soiled dove like her.

"God saw what happened to you," Rachel continued gently. "He sees every moment of pain. Every moment you were powerless. And it grieves Him. He doesn't look at you and see someone tainted or damaged. He sees someone He loves. Someone precious to Him."

The words landed like stones in still water, creating ripples Belle couldn't control.

All the emotion she'd tamped down to be able to tell her story overflowed. She felt herself unraveling and didn't want to do it here.

"I'm going to turn in." The pup made a noise when Belle stood. Cradling the animal to her chest, she murmured goodnight to Rachel, brushed past Coop.

She ducked into the tent, put the pup down, and buried her face in her hands.

Rachel was wrong. God didn't see Belle. She couldn't rely on Him at all.

And she was just fooling herself if she thought she could trust Coop.

He might seem different, but likely he was the same underneath. She couldn't stay married to him. Couldn't give him control.

And she wouldn't trust a God who would only punish someone like her.

Chapter Ten

Dawn had just broken when Belle started putting away the tent. Nearby, the pup wrestled with a piece of cloth Paul and Alex had tied into a knot for her.

The light was gray and misty, casting everything in soft shadows. Cold bit at Belle's cheeks and fingertips despite the gloves she wore. She'd already dressed in her cowboy clothes —the borrowed men's shirt and trousers that had become more familiar than skirts over the past weeks. More practical.

She worked methodically, breaking down the canvas shelter she and Coop had been sharing. It had become routine now. Coop on one side, her on the other, the knife still under her pillow. But she hadn't reached for it in days.

Movement caught her eye. Coop slipped into camp from the direction of the cattle, his silhouette dark against the pale morning light.

Belle crossed to the fire and pulled the coffeepot off of the fading coals. She filled a mug and turned to offer it to him.

That's when she saw it. A smear of blood at the corner of his lip.

"What happened?" The words came out sharper than she'd intended.

Coop's hand went to his mouth, wiped the blot away. "Came off my horse during watch."

Something wasn't right. The way he wouldn't quite meet her eyes. The tension in his shoulders. Was he lying?

Belle wanted to push. Wanted to demand the truth. But she didn't have that right, did she? They were friends. Not husband and wife. Not really.

Even if her heart had become confused lately.

"Coffee's hot," she said instead, pushing it into his hands.

Coop barely looked up as he shoveled the breakfast Alice had left for him into his mouth. The pup ambled over to him and attempted to put both front paws on his knee.

"You want that?" He fed her a bit of egg, speaking in a voice Belle had never heard from him. High-pitched and affectionate. "You're growing so fast. Need all the food you can get."

Even though he was teasing with the pup, he was more subdued than usual. And a part of Belle wanted to cheer him up.

"I've decided on a name," she said quietly. "For the puppy."

He tipped his head toward her. Listening.

"Birdie," she said. "Because she can't help herself from chasing anything with feathers."

He looked up at her and grinned. The expression made him look younger. Lighter. "It suits her."

Belle's stomach did a slow flip.

His smile made the warm feeling in Belle's belly intensify until it became unsettling and confusing. She ducked her head and bent to pick up the tent poles to stow them.

She didn't know what to do with these feelings. Had been trying to keep things at the friendship level, trying not to think about more than that. But Coop's siblings had made her feel like she could be part of their family. Alice teaching her to cook. Collin teasing her like a sister. Even Leo had been less hostile lately.

Everything was getting muddled, the lines she'd drawn so carefully blurring at the edges.

Paul came along to collect Birdie, and Belle followed Coop to the picketed horses.

"Do you need to rest a bit before we get moving for the day?" Belle asked.

Coop shook his head, squinting in the morning sun like his head hurt.. "I'm fine."

Another lie. But Belle didn't confront him.

They mounted up and joined the other cowboys as the wagon train began its morning departure. The terrain had changed over the past days—rockier now, more treacherous. A river wove in and out of the forested area alongside the trail, its water dark and swift. The path was narrow here, forcing the cattle to follow in a contained stream behind the wagons instead of spreading out the way they usually did.

Fine snowflakes started falling. Sharp little crystals that stung when they hit exposed skin. The clouds hung low and heavy in the sky, pressing down like a weight.

"I don't like the look of those clouds." Coop reined in nearby.

Matt was also in earshot. "You think the storm's gonna worsen?"

Coop's gaze scanned the sky. "Hollis might call an early stop today if it gets bad enough."

Matt pushed ahead.

"Stay close," Coop said. "If it gets worse, we won't be able to see far ahead."

Daisy felt familiar beneath her now. She knew the horse, and the horse knew her.

Belle had been thinking about horses a lot lately. How was she going to take care of her cattle without a horse of her own? She had no money to buy one.

The thought brought all her uncertainties rushing back. How was she going to manage a herd alone?

What if one of the cows got injured? What happened at calving time?

Belle pushed the thoughts away and focused on the work. The cattle moved steadily up the rocky trail, their breath creating clouds in the cold air. The cowboys called and whistled to one another, voices carrying across the slender path.

Something was different today. Belle noticed it in the way the men were positioned. A couple of extra riders she didn't recognize worked with them. They were more watchful. Was it only because of the snow?

The herd spread out as the trail widened slightly. Belle found herself pushed toward the edge of the rocky terrain, where the ground dropped away into a ravine. The river rushed at the bottom, loud and angry.

Coop rode a dozen yards behind her. Belle could sense

his presence without looking. Always there. Always watching.

The ground beneath Daisy's hooves shifted slightly. Gravel giving way. The horse side-stepped nervously.

"Be careful up there!" Coop called out.

Belle waved him off. She was fine. Daisy was sure-footed. They'd navigated worse terrain than this.

But then the crack of a gunshot echoed off the rocky ridge across the ravine.

For one frozen moment, Belle didn't understand what she'd heard. The sound was wrong. Distorted by distance and the rocky walls.

Then something hissed into the ground a few feet in front of Daisy.

A bullet. Someone had shot—

The horse spooked.

Reared.

Belle's weight shifted backward. Her hands scrambled for purchase on the reins, but they slipped through her fingers.

"Belle!" Coop's shout rang out behind her.

The world tilted. Daisy's front hooves pawed at the air. Belle grabbed desperately—one hand finding the horse's mane, the other clutching the saddle horn.

Someone was shooting at her.

Sarge. It had to be Sarge.

The cattle milled nervously, their lowing turning anxious. They scattered, moving away from the spooked horse.

Daisy came down hard, her hooves skidding on the loose gravel. The horse sidestepped, trying to find solid ground.

And Belle lost her grip.

She flew backward off the saddle. Her body hit the rocky hillside hard, knocking the air from her lungs. The world spun—sky, rocks, trees, all blurring together.

Belle scrabbled for purchase. Her hands found only loose gravel and small stones that gave way beneath her weight.

She was sliding.

Hooves pounded, coming toward her.

Coop. She sensed more than saw him, heard the desperation in his voice as he shouted her name.

But she couldn't stop her momentum. Couldn't find anything solid to grab onto.

The edge of the ravine rushed up to meet her.

And then there was nothing beneath her at all.

Just air.

And the terrible sensation of falling.

Belle's scream caught in her throat as she plummeted downward.

A second gunshot echoed off the rocks.

Belle fell.

Coop didn't think. Didn't hesitate.

He kicked Scout hard, sent the horse charging toward where Belle had disappeared over the edge of the ravine.

"Belle!"

The rocky ground crumbled beneath Scout's hooves. Too steep. Too unstable. But Coop kept driving the horse forward, because Belle was down there and he would *not* lose her.

Scout's hooves skidded. The horse fought to stay upright, but gravity and momentum pulled them both down the rocky slope toward the dark water rushing below.

Coop saw Belle hit the river. Saw the current swallow her.

Then Scout was in the water too, the cold a physical blow that drove the air from Coop's lungs.

So cold it burned.

The current grabbed at Coop's clothes. Scout kicked, trying to find solid ground. Coop lost his seat, torn from the saddle by the force of the raging river.

Water closed over his head.

The current pulled him below the surface. Tumbled him until he couldn't tell which way was up.

His lungs screamed for air.

He kicked hard. Fought toward what he hoped was the surface.

His head broke through.

He gasped, dragged in a desperate breath that hurt with cold. Snow fell harder now, thick flakes that made it hard to see. The water churned around him, trying to pull him under again.

There.

Belle. Downstream. One hand flailing above the water.

Coop swam. Hard. The current helped him gain on her then pulled him away at the last second. He kept fighting. Nothing mattered except reaching her. Nothing else existed except Belle, and the water, and the desperate need to get to her before she sank under.

His fingers found her arm. Grabbed. Held.

His other arm locked around her waist and pulled her against him.

She was barely moving. Her lips were blue around the edges.

"I've got you!" Coop shouted over the roar of the river. "Can you kick?"

He had to get them out of the water. Had to get them to shore.

But the current was so strong. Pulling them downstream. It slammed his back against rocks that jutted up through the churning rapids. He gasped against the pain.

He held Belle with one arm and stroked toward the bank with the other. His muscles screamed. His body was going numb from the cold. But he would not let go of Belle. Would not lose his grip on her no matter what the river did to them.

The water fought him for every inch. Coop's vision started to blur at the edges. Blackness crept in. He was so cold. The icy, churning water was stealing his strength.

Just a little farther.

A little more.

There—a piece of rocky bank jutting out into the water.

Coop kicked hard one last time. His feet found the river bottom. He lurched forward, pulling Belle with him, half-dragging her through the shallows and up onto the rocks.

They collapsed on the bank. Gasping. Shaking.

The icy wind hit immediately. It bit straight through his soaked clothes and into his bones.

Belle shivered so hard her whole body shook. Coop could feel his own muscles starting to seize up from the cold.

This was dangerous. They were both soaked to the skin. The snow was coming down harder now, thick and heavy.

Hypothermia could set in in minutes. They'd be dead in less than an hour if Coop didn't get them warm.

And they were out in the open. Exposed. Visible.

Sarge was still out there somewhere.

"Did you see where the shots came from?" Coop forced the words out through chattering teeth.

Belle shook her head, her eyes dark and fearful. "S-Sarge." Her jaw trembled so hard she could barely speak.

Water dripped from her hair, already starting to freeze. Coop could barely feel his fingers now.

Movement in the trees.

On instinct, Coop shifted to shield Belle with his body, putting himself between her and whatever was coming through the woods.

A shadow emerged from the trees.

Scout.

Relief hit Coop so hard his knees nearly buckled. The horse was soaked, skin quivering, but alive.

Coop whistled. The sound came out weak, but Scout's ears pricked forward. The horse picked his way carefully down to the rocky bank.

"D-Daisy." Belle's voice was barely a whisper. "Is—is she—?"

Coop remembered seeing Belle's horse get hit when that first shot rang out. "Hit in the flank. Not a shot that would kill her. She'll probably circle back to the herd. One of the cowboys will help her."

Belle made a sound that was half-sob, half-gasp. Tears

spilled down her cheeks, mixing with the river water still dripping from her face.

She cared about that horse. Coop could see it in the way her whole body shook with more than just cold.

But they didn't have time for this.

"We have to get warm." Coop grabbed Belle's shoulders, made her look at him. "We have to get these wet clothes off. We can't stay out here. The snow is worsening. Do you understand?"

Belle nodded, but her eyes were wild.

Coop looked around, trying to orient himself. The river had carried them downstream. How far? A half mile? More? When they'd climbed out, it had been on the opposite side from where the cattle and wagon train had been traveling.

They'd been near the back of the herd when Belle fell. Coop wasn't sure if anyone had seen them go over the edge. Maybe Matt.

Or maybe just Sarge.

Maybe no help was coming.

Scout stamped nervously, his breath visible. The horse was wet but in better shape than either of them.

Coop grabbed Scout's reins and tugged Belle upright. She swayed, nearly fell.

"Come on." Coop pulled her toward the trees. "We have to get into the woods. Can't be out here."

Belle went with him without arguing.

That scared Coop more than anything else.

Belle always argued. Or asked questions. But now she just followed, stumbling over the rocks, her hand clutching his arm.

She was in worse shape than he'd thought.

The woods offered some shelter from the wind and snow. Coop led them deeper into the trees, Scout's reins in hand.

They had to find shelter. Had to get out of these wet clothes. Had to get warm somehow or they were both going to die out here.

Coop's mind raced, trying to think through the cold and exhaustion. His body was starting to shut down. He could feel it—that creeping numbness that meant danger.

Coop scanned the trees, looking for anything. A fallen log. An overhang. A cave. Anything that could offer shelter.

There—a rocky outcropping with a deep overhang. Not perfect, but it would block the wind and snow.

"Almost there." Coop half-carried Belle toward it. "Just a little farther."

She didn't respond. Just kept moving because he was moving her.

They reached the rocky awning, and Coop got Belle down into the sheltered space. The ground was dry here—protected from the snow by the shelf above.

Coop's hands shook as he fumbled with Scout's saddle. Had to get into the saddle bags. Find the flint and steel. But his fingers were so numb he could barely work the buckles.

Frustrated, he managed to wrench them open. He rifled through the contents until he found his tools.

"We're going to be okay." Coop told her over his shoulder. "I'm going to get us warm. Just hold on."

It took too long to get the fire going. Everything was damp. Finally, he had a small flame licking through the tinder.

When he went to her, Belle had curled into herself, arms

wrapped tight around her body. Her eyes were closed. She'd stopped shivering.

"Belle." Coop grabbed her shoulders, shook her gently. "Belle, stay with me. Stay awake."

Leo watched it happen in fragments.

The shot echoing off the rocks. Belle's horse rearing. Belle thrown from the saddle, sliding down the rocky slope toward the ravine.

And Coop—

Coop didn't hesitate. Didn't even slow down. Just kicked Scout hard and rode straight over the edge after her.

"No!" The word ripped out of Leo's throat.

He spurred his own horse into a gallop. Collin was beside him, maybe half a length behind. The ground was treacherous—loose gravel, snow falling harder—but Leo didn't slow down.

"Rusty! Matt!" Leo shouted to the two cowboys nearby. "Push the cattle forward! Everyone stay alert!"

His heart hammered against his ribs. Where would the next shot go? There should be another. Sarge was out there somewhere with a rifle, and Leo had positioned Coop and Belle exactly where he'd wanted them.

Right where Sarge could take a shot.

The plan had been simple. Draw Sarge out. Have the men positioned to take him down the moment he revealed himself.

But Gerry Bones hadn't fired in time.

"Where'd he go?" Leo yelled to Lucky and Owen, who flanked them. "Can we get across the river?"

Leo and Collin reached the edge of the ravine just in time to see Coop hit the water.

The river was raging. Dark and fast and deadly cold.

Coop was on Scout, still mounted, fighting to keep the horse upright in the current. Then a surge of water caught them both. Coop went under.

Leo's stomach dropped.

Come on. Swim.

Coop's head broke the surface.

Then the river swept them both around a bend and out of sight.

"We need to go after him." Collin was already turning his horse, looking for a way down the steep embankment.

Leo's mind was racing. Calculating. The terrain was too steep here. If they tried to ride down, they'd end up in the river themselves. And the snow was getting worse by the minute—thick flakes that made it hard to see more than twenty feet ahead.

"Conditions are getting worse," Leo said. "We've gotta find a better place to get down to the riverbank."

Lucky came racing back, his horse breathing hard. "With the snow falling, we'll lose the trail. Tracks'll be covered over in fifteen minutes."

Collin wheeled his horse around to face Leo. "Why did you have them riding at the back of the company?" His voice was sharp and accusing. "Belle and Coop should have been near the wagons. Protected."

Leo's jaw went tight. "I thought we could get him."

Collin stared at him. "Him? Sarge?" Realization dawned. "You used her as bait."

"Gerry almost had a shot. Rusty was supposed to be closer, but the cattle got spooked by the snow."

How long could someone survive in water that cold?

Minutes. Maybe.

Everything had gone wrong. Every single piece of Leo's carefully constructed plan had fallen apart.

Leo's chest felt like it was being crushed in a vise.

This wasn't supposed to happen.

It's possible I just killed my brother.

All because Leo thought he could manage it. Make it work according to his plan.

Anger surged through Leo. His plan had failed, but this was Coop's fault in the first place. If Coop could once—just once—follow orders...

"Leo." Collin's voice cut through his spiraling thoughts. "What do we do?"

Leo forced himself to come back to the moment. "You search for a crossing. I'm going after Sarge."

"Leo, you can't go alone—"

"It's time to end this." His words brooked no argument, and he rode off into the snow.

Chapter Eleven

Belle's thoughts moved sluggishly. Like wading through mud.

Coop held her by the shoulders and shook her. Had he said something?

How was Coop still moving? He should be as frozen as she was. Should be just as slow, just as disoriented. But his arm came around her waist, supporting her weight when she would have fallen.

Her mind felt disconnected from her body.

"S-Sarge." The word came out through clacking teeth. "He's out there."

"He'll have to go through me to get to you."

Had her eyes closed?

"Belle!"

She smiled. He sounded so worried.

"What?" she managed to ask.

Coop's throat worked. "We have to get undressed. As

much as we can. The wet clothes will keep the cold in. We'll get hypothermia."

He was right. She already felt blackness closing in.

If anyone else had asked her to undress, she would have rejected the idea outright. Would have fought. Would have run.

But this was Coop.

"Okay." But when she bent to pull off her boots, her fingers wouldn't work. They felt thick and clumsy. Foreign.

She got one boot off. Started on the second, but it wouldn't budge. She wobbled and nearly fell. Straightened to attempt the buttons on her shirt, but they were impossibly small. Too difficult.

Belle sat down fully to work at the boots. Maybe if she sat still for a moment, she'd warm up. She was starting to feel warmer already. That was good, wasn't it?

Maybe she should close her eyes. Just for a moment.

Hands grabbed her shoulders. Shook her. Rough.

"Hey!" Belle tried to protest, but the word came out slurred.

"You gotta stay awake." Coop's face was close to hers, his eyes dark and intense. "You've gotta get up."

Belle wanted to argue. But she didn't have the energy for it.

She struggled to her feet. The buttons on her shirt still defeated her frozen fingers.

"I need help." The admission came out quiet. Ashamed.

Coop came to her immediately.

He'd lost his hat somewhere—in the river, probably. His dark hair was plastered to his head, still wet. His eyes held something Belle couldn't name as he reached for the buttons on her shirt.

His hands shook. Belle couldn't stop shaking either. The whole world felt like it was trembling.

Coop got a few buttons undone. Then he made a frustrated sound in the back of his throat. "Can you pull it over your head?"

The wet fabric clung to her skin, heavy and cold. She tugged it upward with numb hands and let it fall in a sodden heap. She still wore her underthings—chemise and drawers, both damp but not soaked through like the shirt had been. She definitely couldn't take those off.

Belle turned her head to tell Coop so and found he already had the saddle blanket in his hands. He draped it around her shoulders. "It's damp, but it'll do."

Beneath the blanket, she quickly pulled off her soaked pants.

"Sit as close to the fire as you can bear," he said, nudging her gently toward the growing flames.

Belle sank down near the blaze. The heat felt distant at first, like it couldn't quite reach through the cold wrapped around her bones. Her underclothes were still damp against her skin, but nothing like the shirt and pants had been.

She huddled in the blanket and watched Coop.

He'd taken care of her this entire time. Pulled her from the river. Found shelter. Started the fire. Given her the blanket.

And only now—only after she was settled—did he start working on his own wet clothes.

The skin around Coop's lips was pale, tinged with blue.

He struggled to pull off his boots, his fingers as clumsy as Belle's had been. But he finally got them off, peeled away his soaked socks.

He wore long john pants beneath his trousers, but stripped off his wet shirt. Belle's eyes skittered away from his bare torso automatically. But not before she'd seen the scars scattered across his chest and shoulders. Old wounds.

His skin was red from the cold. He was in worse shape than he'd let on.

And he'd given her the only blanket.

"You take the blanket." Belle's voice came out as barely a whisper. She'd meant the words to have more volume and conviction.

Coop shook his head as he laid their clothes on the rocky ground near the fire.

"Coop." Belle tried again.

He shook his head even more adamantly. "There's no way on earth I'm taking that blanket from you."

He knelt across the fire from her and fed more sticks into the flames. It was bigger now, putting out real heat, while the falling snow made everything around them quiet. Hushed. Almost private, like they were the only two people left in the world.

Belle couldn't stop watching him. The way his hands flexed, stiff with cold. The careful way he moved, like everything hurt. The moments in the water were a blur. Had he rammed into something there? She thought so, because he was in pain.

Worry flared in Belle's chest. "If you won't take the blanket, then come over here and share it."

Coop's eyes flicked to hers. His jaw firmed like he was about to argue.

Belle set her chin. "We shared our warmth down in that cave and nothing bad happened."

The words were as much for her own reassurance as for Coop. They could sit close together without it turning dangerous.

Coop's expression softened. He slowly came around the fire, moving carefully, like he was approaching a spooked horse. When he sat on the ground beside her, he left space between them.

Belle was the one who scooted closer. She opened the blanket with one arm, making room. "It won't reach unless we're sitting shoulder to shoulder."

A muscle jumped in Coop's cheek, and his thoughts warred across his features.

"We've got to get closer," she whispered.

She didn't wait for him to decide. Just pressed against him, felt the cold radiating from his skin. He needed this warmth as much as she did.

Coop hesitated, then his arm came around her shoulders. He leaned close, so close that Belle's cheek rested against his shoulder. His jaw settled against the top of her head. As he breathed deeply in and out, a small tension eased from his body.

The blanket tucked around both of them now. Barely big enough, but enough.

"Don't fall asleep." Coop's voice was rough and gravelly.

"I'm not asleep." Belle let her eyes drift closed anyway. Just for a moment. "But maybe you had better talk to me. To keep me awake."

Silence stretched out. The fire crackled. Snow whispered through the trees around them.

Then Coop's jaw moved against the top of her head. Halting words that came slow and careful.

"I was ten when my ma died." His chest rose and fell beneath her cheek. "Sickness. Fever. She was gone in three days."

Belle's heart twisted. Ten years old. Just a child.

Coop shifted slightly, reaching one arm out of the blanket to add another stick to the fire. "Pa had died a couple years before, so when Ma died, it was just us kids. Leo, Alice, me, and Collin."

The firelight flickered across the small clearing and made the shadows deeper.

"Leo was fifteen. Alice thirteen. She took a job as a maid in the Braddock's house. Leo had to be the man of the family. Get work at the mill. Make sure we didn't lose our apartment." Coop's voice went flat. "He was good at taking care of us. Always knew what to do. Always had a plan."

Belle felt Coop's hand flex against her shoulder. Tighten. Then relax.

"I didn't know what to do with—with any of it. The grief. The anger. Ma was just gone, and nothing made sense anymore." Coop drew in a breath. Let it out slowly. "There was this boy at school. Tommy Brennan. He said something about Ma dying. Said she probably deserved it, getting sick like that. Said God was punishing our family."

Belle's eyes opened. She tilted her head and shifted to look up at Coop's face.

His jaw was tight. Eyes fixed on the fire. "I hit him. Gave

him a black eye. Got my own face busted up pretty good in return. But it felt—it felt better than the grief. Better than sitting at home thinking about Ma being gone."

Warmth was creeping back into Belle's body. She started shivering—hard tremors that shook through her whole frame.

Coop hugged her closer. He rubbed her arm slowly, absently.

"Fighting made the pain go away," Coop continued. "At least for a while. The ache in my ribs, the split lip, the black eye—those hurt in ways I could understand. Not like the grief. It was a gaping wound I couldn't see or touch or fix."

He fed another stick to the fire.

Belle's fingertips started to hurt as feeling returned to them in painful prickles that made her wince.

Coop shivered now, too. His body fighting to generate heat.

Telling the story hurt less than Coop had expected.

He usually couldn't stand talking about Ma. About that time with Leo.

But somehow, Belle made it easier.

The way she listened. Quiet. Still. Just the small movement of her head against his shoulder. The warmth of her cheek pressed to his neck. Like she was there with him in that memory. Like she could see the ten-year-old boy who'd been so desperate to escape his grief that he'd broken another kid's nose just to feel something that wasn't the unbearable weight of loss.

Coop drew in a breath. Made himself finish.

"Leo demanded I stop fighting. Like it was just that easy. Maybe he never thought I tried to stop, but I did."

Belle shifted slightly against him, settling closer.

"The drinking started when I was about sixteen. It was easier to ignore all the bad things about myself when I'd had a few drinks."

It had never made them go away. He'd always known he was what Leo said. A failure. Stupid.

"But the whiskey sometimes fueled more fights. A friend told me I could get paid to box—if I won. I did that sometimes. Got paid to take a beating. None of it helped. Not really."

He fed another stick to the fire. Watched it catch and flare.

"When Oliver and Tann died, I was at my lowest. For a long time... I wanted to die, too."

It was true. He'd thought that death would mean oblivion, that whatever came after had to be better than the grief, better than the emptiness...

Belle's hand moved. Found his where it rested against her arm. Her fingers threaded through his.

He'd almost accomplished it. That night, weeks ago, he'd been drunk and stupid and almost drowned himself in that creek. But Belle had pulled him out. And even through his drunken haze, something had changed the moment he'd seen her.

He didn't want to die.

He wanted to live. For her.

He didn't know if he should tell her that. His chest felt hollow and raw. Everything laid bare.

Belle was quiet for a long time. So long that Coop started to worry he'd said too much. What would she think of him now?

Finally, she spoke, "Rachel told me something a few nights ago. From the Bible. I didn't realize it at the time, but I think she was trying to tell me—well, she said, 'The Lord's mercies are new every morning.' From Lamentations, I...I think."

New every morning.

Something hot and big lodged in Coop's chest at the words.

"I didn't really understand it at the time," Belle continued. "But I think—I think it means that God doesn't keep score the way people do. That every morning, He offers new mercy. Not based on what you did yesterday. Not based on how many times you failed."

Hearing the words felt like experiencing the instant he'd gone into the river after Belle all over again. The icy blast had stolen his breath, frozen everything for one singular moment.

Her head moved against his shoulder, her cheek pressing into his skin for a brief moment as she settled. His heart was nearly pounding out of his chest—could she hear it?

"Leo keeps score," Belle said quietly. "But maybe God doesn't. Maybe His love isn't like Leo's approval. Maybe it's—maybe it's something different entirely."

Coop couldn't find words for the feeling expanding in his chest. Hope and grief and longing, all mixed up.

God's mercies, new every morning.

It was the exact opposite of everything Coop had been told all his life. Everything he believed.

"I think you're a good man, Coop."

The words punched straight through him. Stole his breath so he couldn't answer. His heart was acting strange in his chest. Expanding. Aching. Filling with a hope so fierce it hurt.

Belle's breathing started to even out. Grow slow and deep. A knot of worry twisted in his belly, but he realized that it was all right. They'd both warmed up, sitting close together by the fire. No doubt she was exhausted from fighting against the river.

She dozed off, warm and safe against his side, while he kept watch.

Now that she was asleep, Coop looked down at her. At the woman who'd told him he was good.

He wanted to be worthy of her belief. Wanted to be the man she saw when she looked at him.

But first, he had to get Belle back to camp. Keep her safe from Sarge.

Then he would figure out how to get out from under Larson's thumb. Pay back the debt. Cut the ties.

Then, only then, would he ask Belle to give their marriage a chance.

His own eyes started to grow heavy. But something else niggled at him. Something that didn't quite fit.

Why had he and Belle been assigned to ride at the back of the herd this morning? He'd gotten word of their assignment from Rusty. Hadn't questioned it at the time. He'd been up in his head about Larson, deep in guilt for what he'd already done on the man's behalf. Hadn't given half a thought to the idea that he and Belle would be farthest away from the safety of the wagons.

Why would Leo want them at the back of the herd? Exposed?

Suspicion sparked inside Coop, but he stamped it out.

Now wasn't the time. He had one job ahead of him: get Belle back to the wagons.

Whatever it took.

Chapter Twelve

Hours had passed. The snow continued to fall in thick, steady curtains around their shelter, muffling all sound beyond the rocky overhang. Coop had been feeding the fire carefully, keeping it alive without letting it grow too large. The flames cast flickering light across the small space, painting everything in shades of gold and shadow. The shelter wasn't deep—maybe six feet at most—but the overhang protected them from the worst of the wind and snow. Stone walls radiated a faint warmth where the firelight touched them.

He checked their clothes again. Spread across flat rocks near the flames, the fabric had finally dried—mostly. Belle's shirt and trousers were stiff in places, where the river water had frozen before the heat could reach it, but they were wearable. His own shirt and trousers felt almost normal again.

Coop gathered Belle's things and moved toward where

she sat wrapped in the saddle blanket. "Here. They're dry enough now."

Belle took the clothes from him, but her eyes were worried. "I think Sarge is still out there."

"Maybe." Coop kept his voice calm. "But the snow is gonna make it a lot harder for anybody to travel through it, on horse or by foot."

He gestured to where the snow had already accumulated several inches deep beyond their sheltered space. The world outside their small circle of firelight had gone white and silent. Wind moaned through the pine trees higher up the slope, shaking loose small avalanches of snow from laden branches.

"And I think the snow is probably hiding our smoke," Coop added. "Making it hard for anyone to track us. We were in the river for quite a bit—that likely put a good distance between us and whoever was shooting."

"What about Daisy?"

"Leo and the men will have taken care of her. Your horse is valuable—part of the herd. They won't have left her."

Belle nodded. She shivered despite the warmth from the fire. "I'm not looking forward to crossing the river again."

Coop moved closer, crouched down so they were eye level. "We'll try and find a place with a lot more gentle crossing. Somewhere the current isn't so strong. We won't do it the way we did before—I promise you that."

Belle's expression shifted into something soft and serious at the same time.

"You saved my life," she said.

Coop held her gaze. "I would do it all over again. All of it."

The meaning hung between them. Not just saving her from the river. But all of it. Being with her. Protecting her. Choosing her.

She looked down at the clothing in her hands. "I should—I should change."

"Right." Coop stood quickly. Grabbed the saddle blanket from around her shoulders and held it up high, stretched between his outstretched arms above the level of his head. A makeshift privacy screen. "I won't look."

He turned his face away, kept his eyes fixed on the rocky wall of the overhang while Belle moved behind the blanket. He heard the rustle of fabric. The soft sounds of her dressing. Outside, Scout stamped and shifted, shaking snow from his mane.

Coop kept his gaze averted. Kept his word.

When Belle said, "Okay," Coop lowered the blanket.

She stood a few feet away, back in Stella's disguise. It was wrinkled and stiff, but she was covered. Her coat lay near the fire—the leather frozen through in spots.

Coop quickly pulled on his own shirt. The fabric was warm from the fire, almost comfortable. He left his coat where it was—not quite dry yet—and moved to wrap the blanket around Belle's shoulders again.

She stood still while he settled it around her.

They stood face to face. Almost nose to nose. Close enough that Coop could see the way her eyelashes cast shadows on her cheeks in the firelight. Could see the faint freckles across the bridge of her nose that he'd never noticed before. Her breath made small clouds in the cold air between them.

His hand moved without permission. Reached up.

Touched her hair with the tips of his fingers—so gently it was barely contact at all.

"Your hair is dry," he whispered.

He couldn't think of anything else to say after that. Couldn't think at all with Belle this close. With the firelight caught in her eyes and the soft curve of her mouth just inches from his.

They were breathing the same air. Sharing the same space.

Coop's eyes dropped to her lips. He wanted to kiss her, wanted it more than he'd ever wanted anything in his entire life. Wanted to close that small distance. Wanted to feel her mouth against his. Wanted to know if she'd kiss him back or pull away.

But wanting something didn't give him the right to take it.

Coop stepped back. Dropped his hand. Ran his fingers through his own hair instead, trying to redirect the energy thrumming through his body.

He turned away. Grabbed his gloves from where they were drying near the fire and checked—still damp. He set them back down.

Belle sat back down by the fire. Coop heard the soft rustle of the blanket settling around her.

"I think you might be the only man who hasn't tried to take a kiss from me."

The words hit Coop like a fist to the gut. He squatted by the fire, his back half-turned to Belle. He fed a few more sticks into the flames. Found himself grateful for the task—something to do with his hands. The fire popped and crackled, sending up small showers of sparks that died against the stone ceiling.

He'd found a treasure trove of mostly dry wood beneath a windfall earlier. Enough to keep the fire going through the night if they were careful.

"A kiss is no good if it has to be taken." His voice came out rougher than he'd intended. "I would only want a kiss from my wife if it was freely given."

He was careful not to say Belle's name. Just *my wife*.

Because that's what she was, wasn't she? At least for now. At least until they reached Oregon and the arrangement ended.

Coop glanced at Belle from the corner of his eye. She sat very still, her expression thoughtful.

The fire crackled. Snow whispered through the trees beyond their shelter. The temperature was dropping as night deepened—Coop could feel it creeping into their small space despite the fire's warmth.

Coop fed another stick to the flames and tried not to hope too hard that his words mattered to her.

"It's coming on to nightfall," Coop said. "Anybody searching for us isn't gonna try and continue in these dangerous conditions. Not in this snow. Not in the dark."

Belle hugged the blanket tighter around herself. "Sarge might."

"Maybe." Coop kept his tone calm. "But even Sarge has to be smart. Can't track what he can't see. Can't cross a river he can't navigate safely."

He looked at Belle directly now. "I think we should try and get some rest. Sleep for a few hours. Hopefully, the snow will slow, and we can find a good crossing in the morning. Get back to camp."

Belle nodded slowly. Then, to Coop's surprise, she shifted closer to him. Not reluctantly. Not with the wariness he'd grown used to.

Willing.

Belle settled against his side, and Coop wrapped his arm around her shoulders. Pulled her close. Shared his warmth the way they had earlier.

Then Belle reached for his hands.

Coop's breath caught. His chapped, raw hands that had been in the freezing water too long.

She gently chafed them between her own smaller ones. Rubbing warmth into his cold fingers. Taking care of him.

It was the first time Belle had initiated touch between them. The first time she'd reached for him instead of just accepting his touch.

Coop stared down at their joined hands and something vast and terrifying opened up in his chest.

He wanted more time. Wanted more days on this trail. More nights around campfires. More moments when Belle chose to be close to him.

But Oregon was close now. Maybe three days. Maybe four, if the snow delayed them.

Belle tipped her head against Coop's shoulder. Her breathing began to even out. Slow and deep. Drifting toward sleep.

Coop looked down at her. At the woman who was so completely different from the terrified, knife-wielding stranger he'd fallen into a cave with weeks ago.

Back then, she'd jumped every time he'd touched her.

Flinched away. Pulled a weapon. Looked at him like he was another threat she had to survive.

Now she chose to lean against him. Chose to let him hold her. Chose to touch him first.

He'd earned a modicum of her trust. Maybe more than a modicum.

And maybe it made Coop a selfish fool, but he wanted more. Wanted all of it. Wanted her to choose him not just for tonight, but for all the nights after.

The fire flickered and danced, throwing their shadows against the stone wall. Scout stamped outside their shelter, snow accumulating on his back in a thick white blanket. The horse had his head down, resting but alert, one ear swiveled toward the darkness.

The exhaustion from fighting the river—from pulling Belle to safety, from building the fire, from keeping watch—it all caught up with Coop at once. Combined with the warmth from the flames and the solid weight of Belle against his side, his eyes drifted closed.

Just for a moment, he told himself. Just a moment to rest.

But sleep pulled at him. Insistent. Irresistible.

Coop's last conscious thought was a prayer he didn't quite know how to form. Something about time. About second chances. About being given more days to prove himself.

About Belle choosing to stay.

Then he dozed off with Belle warm and safe in his arms and the fire burning steady against the darkness beyond.

Coop's body jerked.

Belle startled awake, disoriented in the darkness. For a moment, she couldn't remember where she was. The rocky overhang. The dying fire. The wilderness.

The snow had stopped. Everything was quiet—impossibly quiet, the way the world went silent after fresh snowfall. Only the tiny crackles from the fire broke the stillness. The flames had burned down to glowing coals that cast barely any light.

Belle was warm, cocooned in the blanket with Coop, his body heat wrapped around her. An inch of snow sat on top of the blanket, but somehow it didn't make them cold. Just insulated them further in their tiny shelter.

Coop jerked again. His face was drawn tight, features twisted in what Belle recognized as a nightmare.

But she didn't feel scared of Coop anymore.

She knew he was hurting. Knew his past haunted him the way hers haunted her.

Belle curled closer instead of pulling away. Wrapped her arms more firmly around his torso. Laid her cheek against his chest, right over his heart.

The steady thump-thump beneath her ear was reassuring.

Coop's breathing changed. Became less ragged. He was waking up.

"Sorry." His voice came out rough. Thick with sleep. "I'm sorry. Another nightmare. I woke you up."

Belle stayed pressed against his chest. "I have nightmares, too."

Coop's hand moved, rested lightly on her back.

"No." Belle drew in a breath. Let it out slowly. "From a long time ago."

Coop went very still. Listening. Waiting.

And Belle found herself wanting to tell him. Needing to tell him.

The words came slowly.

"We lived an isolated life. My father was a trapper." Belle's voice sounded strange to her own ears. Distant. "We had a small dugout. Out in the wilderness. Just the three of us—my father, my mother, and me."

The fire crackled softly. A log settled deeper into the coals.

"My father spent most of his time outside. Setting traps. Checking his lines. My mother did the tanning. Got the pelts ready to trade or sell." Belle could see it in her mind. The tiny space. The smell of smoke and cured leather. Her mother's hands always working. "I helped her when I was old enough."

Coop's thumb moved in a gentle circle against her back. Encouraging without pushing.

"When my mother got sick—" Belle's throat tightened. "My father changed. He was harsh with me. Angry all the time. I wouldn't have realized it at the time, but looking back, I think he was scared of losing her."

The memory was so clear. Sharp-edged and painful.

"One day I spilled some water. Just an accident. I was trying to help, trying to bring her a drink, and my hands were too small or too clumsy. The cup fell." Belle's voice went small. Thin. "My father backhanded me across the face."

She could still feel the shock of it. The way her cheek had stung. The ringing in her ears.

"It knocked me to the ground. I just—I remember lying there, tasting blood, and my mother was too weak to get out of bed to help me. And I realized—" Belle's chest went tight. "If I wasn't safe at home with the people who were meant to love me and provide for me, when would I ever be safe?"

The question had followed Belle her whole life. Through her father's death. Through her uncle's betrayal. Through every moment in the brothel.

If home wasn't safe, nowhere was safe.

Belle hadn't realized until she finished speaking that Coop's arm had curled around her shoulders. Not just holding her for warmth. Embracing her. Hugging her.

Tender. Protective.

And Belle didn't feel frightened. Didn't feel trapped.

She just felt safe.

"Belle." Coop's voice was rough with emotion. "A father's job is to protect his little girl. Take care of his wife. What happened to you wasn't your fault. None of it was your fault."

Coop shifted slightly, settling Belle more securely against him. "When my mother was still alive, we'd read the Bible together every night as a family. Ma would probably be ashamed at how I've walked away from my faith. Or tried to. Could never quite get her voice out of my head."

Coop's chest rose and fell beneath Belle's cheek. She sensed him gathering his thoughts.

"There was a verse she loved. Made us memorize it." Coop's voice went soft. Almost reverent. "Jesus said, 'Come to me, all you who are weary and burdened, and I will give you rest. Take my yoke upon you and learn from me, for I am gentle and humble in heart, and you will find rest for your souls. For my yoke is easy and my burden is light.'"

The words hung in the quiet darkness. Belle let them settle over her. Into her.

Come to me. I will give you rest.

For I am gentle and humble in heart.

My yoke is easy and my burden is light.

It was the opposite of everything Belle had believed about God. About surrender. About what it meant to give control to someone more powerful.

"I've never told anyone that before," Belle whispered. "About my father. About—about what happened."

"I'm honored you told me." Coop's arms tightened around her.

Belle let the scripture sit in her mind. Examined it. Turned it over like a stone in her hand.

She desperately wanted to believe it.

There was a long stretch of quiet. Just breathing. Just heartbeats. Just the soft hiss of dying coals.

Belle was still pressed against Coop's chest. His arms still held her. They were so close. So warm.

She wanted to see his face, so she tipped her head back. Put an inch or two of space between them so she could look up.

Coop's hand moved to cup the back of her head. Gentle. Careful. His thumb brushed against her hair.

In the dim glow from the fire, Belle could just make out his features. The strong line of his jaw. The way he looked at her—like she was precious.

A kiss is no good if it has to be taken. I would only want a kiss from my wife if it was freely given. The words echoed in Belle's memory.

Coop had become so dear to her. This man who'd saved her life. Who'd listened to her darkest stories. Who'd held her without taking. Who'd given her space to choose.

Belle reached up. Brushed some hair back from his forehead with gentle fingers.

Coop didn't move. Didn't react. Just let her do what she wanted. Let her touch him without expectation.

She ran her fingertips across his brow. Just above his eyebrow. Down his cheek, feeling the roughness of stubble. She cupped his jaw, felt the warmth of his skin beneath her palm.

Then, completely of her own volition, Belle leaned up and kissed him.

Time slowed. Stopped. The whole world narrowed to just this—her lips against his.

Coop was barely breathing. Belle could sense it. Could feel the way he'd gone absolutely still. Like he was afraid any movement might break the spell.

Belle had experienced hundreds of kisses. Maybe thousands. But never like this.

Never willingly. Never as a participant instead of a victim.

She took in everything. The softness of his lips. The way his nose brushed against her cheek. The warmth of his breath mingling with hers. When she drew back slightly—just a fraction—the gentle puff of air from his exhale ghosted across her lips.

He was like a statue. Frozen.

Belle brushed one more gentle kiss across his mouth. Soft. Tender. Hers to give.

Then heat flooded her cheeks. A terrible blush that made her face burn.

Belle ducked her head, rested it back on Coop's shoulder. Her heart was beating so loud in her ears she could barely hear anything else.

Coop didn't say anything. The blanket had slipped from Belle's shoulder, and he carefully pulled it back up. Settled her close against him.

He didn't ask for more. Didn't take. Didn't demand.

Belle could hear his heart pounding in his chest beneath her ear. But he just held her. Nothing else.

And Belle couldn't stop thinking about the deal they'd made.

She'd given him this kiss. She had feelings for him—feelings different than anything she'd ever felt before. So—what did it mean for their arrangement?

They were supposed to split the cattle in Oregon. Go their separate ways. That was the deal.

But she had just kissed him. Had chosen to kiss him. Had wanted to kiss him.

What did that mean?

Uncertainty churned in Belle's stomach. Confusion tangled with something warmer. Something that felt dangerously close to hope.

But even with all the uncertainty, Belle couldn't regret the kiss.

It had been hers. Her choice.

She felt Coop's chin rest gently on top of her head. Felt the steady rise and fall of his breathing.

She closed her eyes. Tried to let go of all the tangled thoughts. All the questions about what this meant and what came next.

In the morning, they'd have to find a way back across the river. Have to race to catch up with the wagon train. Have to face whatever came next.

But for now, Belle let herself rest against Coop's chest.

Sleep pulled at her, gentle and insistent. And she let herself drift, warm and safe, with Coop's arms around her and the memory of her first freely given kiss still tingling on her lips.

Chapter Thirteen

Voices carried across the frigid morning air.

In the saddle, with Belle behind him, Coop's hand went immediately to his rifle. He drew it from the scabbard with practiced ease, eyes scanning the opposite bank of the river where the sounds came from.

The snow had stopped sometime before dawn, but everything was white and still. Fresh powder covered the ground, muffling sound, transforming the landscape into something clean and unmarked.

Coop and Belle had been riding for over an hour, searching for a safe crossing. Scout moved beneath them with steady patience, despite carrying double. The horse had survived yesterday's ordeal better than either of his riders had any right to expect.

Belle's arms circled his waist. Her cheek pressed against the back of his shoulder.

The trust in that simple gesture made Coop ache.

She'd kissed him. Coop still couldn't quite process it.

The feel of her lips on his. The implied trust.

He'd woken this morning feeling like maybe—just maybe—he had a chance. Like the arrangement between them could become something real.

Like she might choose to stay.

The voices grew louder. He caught movement through the trees on the far bank.

Coop's hand tightened on the rifle. He squeezed Belle's knee gently—a silent signal to be quiet, to stay small behind him.

She stiffened against his back. Alert now. Her arms tightened around his waist.

Riders emerged from the tree line. Matt, Rusty, Collin, and someone else he couldn't see.

Relief crashed through him so hard his shoulders sagged.

"Coop!" Collin's voice rang out across the distance.

Coop's twin kicked his horse into motion, splashing through the shallow crossing Coop and Belle had been approaching. The other three riders followed.

Coop dismounted carefully, mindful of Belle behind him. His legs protested—stiff from the cold and the long night and the river yesterday. But he stayed upright.

Collin hit the ground running. Literally threw himself off his horse before the animal had fully stopped and crashed into Coop with enough force to nearly knock them both over.

Coop grabbed his brother. Held on tight. Let himself feel the relief of being found. Of not being alone in the wilderness anymore.

"You're alive." Collin's voice was thick. "We didn't know—we saw you go over—"

"I'm alright." Coop pulled back enough to look his twin in the face. "We're both alright."

Collin's eyes were red-rimmed. Like he hadn't slept. Or maybe like he'd been crying and didn't want anyone to know it.

The other riders had reached them now. Matt and Rusty, both looking relieved. And—

Larson.

Coop's jaw tightened.

Larson's expression was carefully neutral. But his eyes held something calculating. Something that made the hair on the back of Coop's neck stand up.

"Brought blankets," Rusty said. He dismounted and started pulling supplies from his saddlebags. "And some food. Figured you'd need it."

"Collin." Coop tipped his head. "Can you give some breakfast to Belle first? She needs to eat."

Collin hesitated. His eyes flicked between Coop and Larson. He knew something was going on.

"I'll be right there," Coop said.

Collin squeezed Coop's shoulder once. Hard. Then moved toward where Belle still sat on Scout, looking small and exhausted in the morning light. The other cowboys followed Collin.

Larson dismounted slowly.

Coop walked up to him.

This was it. The bend in the river where the current changed. Where you either committed to crossing or turned back. Where there was no middle ground, no safe harbor, no way to stay in the shallows.

Coop had spent his whole life looking for the easy way

out. But Belle had kissed him last night. Had told him things she'd never told anyone before. Had chosen to trust him with pieces of herself she'd never given anyone.

And Coop was done making wrong choices.

"I'm not going to collect on your debts for you anymore," Coop said. The words came out steady. "It's not right what you're doing to good folks. I won't be a part of it."

Larson's eyes narrowed. A flash of surprise crossed his face—quickly masked, but there.

"May I remind you that you owe me quite a bit of money?" Larson's voice remained pleasant.

"I'm good for it." Coop held the man's gaze. "I'll take whatever job I can find as soon as we get to Oregon. And I will pay you back."

"That might have worked if we had a written agreement." Larson's smile didn't reach his eyes. "But what we've got is a handshake. There were no terms settled in writing. So your plan is not good enough for me."

Heat flared in Coop's chest. Anger he had to fight to keep contained. "It'll have to be good enough for now."

"Will it?" Larson tilted his head. Still smiling that empty smile. "Would you like for me to reveal the way you've been collecting my debts? To Hollis. To your brother." His eyes slid past Coop toward where Belle stood. "To your new wife."

Coop's stomach dropped. His hands clenched into fists.

Telling Hollis would get Coop thrown off the wagon train. Telling Leo would just confirm everything his brother already believed about him—that Coop couldn't be trusted.

But telling Belle—

Telling Belle would destroy everything.

She'd trusted him.

And if she found out?

She'd never look at him the same way again.

"You stay away from my wife." Coop said dangerously. He started to walk away. Toward Belle and Collin. Toward the people who mattered.

"You're gonna regret breaking our deal," Larson called after him.

The words sent a chill down Coop's spine.

He looked at Belle, wrapped in one of the blankets Rusty had brought, holding a piece of bread Collin must have given her. But her eyes were on Coop.

And she smiled. Small. Gentle. Just for him.

Uncertainty churned in his gut.

How could he keep her from finding out? How could he protect what they'd started building between them?

He'd tried everything he could to start a new life. To make a life they could share together. To become the man she believed he was.

But he had a hunch Larson wasn't going to let this go.

What was Coop going to do then?

Collin appeared at his elbow. "You alright?"

"Yeah." The lie tasted bitter. "Let's get Belle back to camp."

"Leo's been searching for you all night," Collin said quietly. "He's out there alone. Looking for Sarge."

Coop's thoughts had been churning all night. He and Belle should never have been in that vulnerable position at the back of the herd. Purposefully or not, Leo had put them in danger.

He would never forgive his brother for nearly getting Belle killed.

As soon as he saw Leo, they would have words.

Belle ducked into the tent. Finally. Privacy. Space to breathe.

And dry clothes.

The men's clothes she'd been wearing had mostly dried by the fire out in the wilderness, but they smelled like smoke and river water. Still felt wrong against her skin.

The disguise didn't matter anymore anyway. Sarge knew. Had figured out it was her. Had taken a shot that sent her tumbling into the ravine.

Belle stripped off the rough shirt and trousers. Reached for her dress. The familiar weight of skirts felt strange after days in men's clothing.

Her hands shook slightly as she fastened the buttons. She couldn't stop thinking about the ride back to camp. About how quiet Coop had been. How there'd seemed to be more distance between them after Collin and the other men found them at the river.

Like something had shifted.

Belle wasn't sure what. Wasn't sure if it was good or bad.

And underneath all of that—underneath the worry about Sarge and the confusion about Coop—there was something else.

Something that surprised Belle.

She didn't feel as scared as she had before.

Before, she'd been completely alone. Facing Sarge and his threats with no one to turn to.

But now—

Now she had Coop. Who'd ridden into a raging river after her. Who'd held her through the night. Who'd listened to her darkest stories and hadn't cast judgment.

Maybe she could lean on him. Just a little.

The thought was terrifying. But also—strange as it seemed—comforting.

Belle finished with the last button on her dress. Started braiding her hair.

Footsteps outside the tent. More than one person. Voices.

Belle froze, heart pounding.

"I don't want you to leave camp for any reason." She recognized Owen's worried voice. "Not to wash up. Not to clean up the breakfast dishes. It's not safe with Sarge out there."

"Clearly, he only wants Belle." Rachel's voice. Arguing but not angry. "She can stay in camp. I should be fine."

"You don't know that." Owen's voice rose slightly. "Sarge is unpredictable. Dangerous. Seems like he'll shoot first and not care who he hits."

"I can handle myself—"

"Rachel." Owen's voice dropped. Went soft in a way that made Belle's chest ache. "I would be lost if something happened to you. You and Molly are everything to me."

Silence. Belle could almost hear Rachel's resolve crumbling.

"It's not ideal," Rachel said finally. Her voice was quiet. "But I will do as you say. I trust your judgment."

More footsteps. Had they both left?

Belle waited a moment. Then pushed through the tent flap.

Rachel was still standing there. Staring after her husband, her expression thoughtful. For once she wasn't carrying the baby.

She startled when Belle emerged. "Oh! I didn't realize you were—"

"I'm sorry." Belle felt heat rise in her cheeks. "I didn't mean to eavesdrop."

Rachel waved a hand. "I've learned there's no real privacy out here on the trail." A small smile touched her lips. "Makes me want my own home even more."

Her own home.

Belle thought about Coop. About how he'd talked about her having a home. Asked her what she might want in it. A big kitchen. A garden. Space to grow things.

For the first time, Belle thought maybe it wouldn't be a bad thing not to be alone.

The thought caught her off guard. Made her breath hitch.

It must have altered her expression because Rachel tilted her head. "Are you alright?"

"I—" The words felt stuck.

Rachel seemed to sense it. "What's on your mind?"

Belle took a breath. Let it out slowly. "Can I ask you something?"

"Of course."

"You said you'd do what Owen wanted. That you trust him." Belle's hands twisted in her skirts. "But you don't have to. You're not—you're not forced to listen to him."

"No." Rachel's expression softened. "I'm not forced."

"But you married him. Promised to obey—Why—" Belle couldn't find the right words.

How could one trust a husband not to use those vows against you?

Rachel seemed to understand. She moved closer. Sat down on a nearby crate. Gestured for Belle to join her.

"Do you know what the Bible says about marriage?" Rachel asked gently.

Belle shook her head.

"In Genesis, it says that a man will leave his father and mother and be joined to his wife. The two become one flesh." Rachel's voice was patient. "And in the New Testament, it says that a husband is supposed to love his wife the way Christ loved the church. Do you know what that means?"

Belle shook her head again.

"It means he's supposed to love her so much that he would die for her." Rachel's eyes were steady. "That's what God asks of husbands. To love their wives sacrificially. Protectively. To put their wives' needs above their own."

That didn't sound right.

"Owen and I don't always see eye to eye," Rachel continued. She shook her head slightly. Got a nostalgic look on her face. "Especially in the very beginning. We fought about everything."

Belle could imagine Rachel—strong, capable Rachel—butting heads with Owen.

"But I've learned something," Rachel said. "I don't have to submit to Owen. I choose to submit to him. Because I know that Owen wants what's best for me. That he wants to keep me safe. That he loves me the way Christ calls him to love me."

She paused. Met Belle's eyes directly. "And if there was ever a situation where I felt strongly enough to argue with him—really argue, not just complain about doing dishes—I believe Owen would listen to me. He would take my input into account when making decisions."

The words clicked into place. Put language to something Belle had been seeing but couldn't name.

This was what she'd witnessed in Coop's family. A give and take. A partnership where one person led but the other wasn't powerless. Wasn't voiceless.

It was so different from what Belle had known.

Her father had been harsh. Angry. Had struck her mother when things went wrong. Had struck Belle.

Her uncle had sold her. Abandoned her to men who used her.

The brothel had been nothing but men taking what they wanted. Using her body.

Belle thought about Coop. About how he'd never taken anything she hadn't offered. How he'd held her without demanding more. How he'd asked what she wanted in a home instead of deciding for her.

What would it look like if they were married for real?

The question rose unbidden. Terrifying. Thrilling.

Could it be real between us?

Belle's chest felt tight. Her hands trembled slightly.

"Thank you," she managed. Her voice came out rough. "For—for explaining."

Rachel smiled. Squeezed Belle's hand briefly. "Anytime."

Alice called Rachel's name. Rachel stood. Squeezed Belle's shoulder once before moving away.

Belle walked to the fire. Poured herself coffee. The tin cup was warm in her hands.

Other people moved through camp. Voices and movement and the regular rhythms of life on the trail. But Belle barely noticed. She sat on a log near the fire. Sipped her coffee. Let her thoughts settle.

Could it be true? Could she be Coop's wife and not lose her freedom? Not lose her very self?

Chapter Fourteen

Coop needed money. A lot. Enough to pay off Larson and end this nightmare.

He'd spent the afternoon swallowing his pride. Going from wagon to wagon. Talking to men he knew had businesses before they'd left on the trail. Asking whether they'd give him a job, give him an advance.

The answers kept coming back the same.

No.

"I need somebody reliable, Spencer." That had been Harrison, who was setting up a freight business. "Can't have someone who might show up drunk. Or not show up at all."

Coop had tried to argue. "I haven't touched a drink since—"

"Since when? Last week? Last month?" Harrison had shaken his head.

He acted like Coop was a child who needed scolding.

Coop had moved on. Tried Fletcher, who was planning to open a mercantile.

"We need people we can trust," Fletcher had said. "No troublemakers. No one who's gonna bring their problems into our business."

Troublemaker. That's what they all thought he was.

Coop walked along the edge of camp now. The wagons were circled for the night. Fires burning. Families gathering for supper.

He was out of time.

He could ask Rob. Rob Braddock had money. He was setting up a sawmill but had lost all his supplies and tools. Now he was in partnership with Leo. They'd need workers.

But the thought turned Coop's stomach.

Going to Rob meant going to Leo. Meant admitting he couldn't handle his own problems. Meant proving—again—that he was the failure his brother believed him to be.

Coop couldn't do it.

So where did that leave him?

He could sell the cattle. Not the ones he'd promised Belle. Split the herd and sell his half. It would give him enough to pay Larson and clear the debt.

But if Belle asked why, he'd have to come clean about his dealings with Larson.

If he sold his cattle, he'd destroy that trust. Destroy any chance they had of making this marriage real.

But if he didn't pay Larson—

Coop's jaw clenched. His hands fisted at his sides.

He was trapped.

Every door had closed. Every option cut off.

Coop rounded the edge of Doc and Maddie's wagon.

The cattle were settled for the night. It was almost his turn for watch.

Movement from behind him.

Coop started to turn.

A fist connected with his jaw. Snapped his head to the side. Stars exploded across his vision.

Coop staggered. Caught his balance before he fell. Raised his hands.

Seth came out of the darkness between the wagons. Two more men right beside him.

Larson's men.

"Hey." Coop backed up a step. "Look, whatever message Larson wants you to deliver, this is between me and him. We can work it out without—"

"You knew better'n to double cross him," Seth said. His smile was all teeth. No warmth. "Boys."

It was an order, and they rushed him.

Coop threw a punch. Connected with someone's face. Felt the satisfying crunch of bone under his knuckles.

But then there were hands grabbing him. Pulling him down.

Coop tried to sidestep. Get away. But someone caught his leg. Yanked.

He went down hard. His shoulder hit first. Then his head.

The world spun.

A boot connected with his ribs. Once. Twice. Pain exploded through his chest. Made it impossible to catch his breath.

Coop tried to roll away. Tried to protect himself.

Hands grabbed his arms. Wrenched them behind his back, pulled him to his knees, head hanging.

"Come on in," one of them said. Laughing. "He ain't gonna fight back now."

A fist slammed into Coop's face. His nose crunched. Blood poured hot and metallic down his lips and chin.

Another punch. This one caught his eye. The socket exploded with pain. His vision went white.

Coop tried to wrench free. Tried to get his arms loose.

But the man holding him was too strong. Too heavy.

Another punch. Coop felt his lip split. Tasted blood.

A knee to his stomach. All the air left his lungs. He couldn't breathe. Couldn't think.

Just pain. Wave after wave of pain.

The beating went on. And on. Fists and boots. Ribs and face and stomach.

Coop couldn't fight anymore. Just tried to breathe. Tried to stay conscious.

He blacked out. Came to again.

Finally, they let him go.

Coop collapsed face-first into the dirt. His whole body screamed.

Footsteps. Someone kicked him once more. In the ribs. Hard enough to make Coop gasp.

"That'll teach him," Seth said.

"Larson's not done with you," another voice added. "Next time he asks for something, you better be prepared to say yes."

Their footsteps faded away.

Coop lay there, gasping for breath.

His ribs were on fire.

Everything hurt.

He tried to push himself up. His arms shook. Gave out. He fell back into the dirt.

He'd accomplished nothing.

He had no money to pay Larson. No job prospects. No way to fix this mess he'd made.

And now Larson's men had made it crystal clear what would happen if Coop didn't do what he was told.

Larson wanted him to be exactly the kind of man Belle had spent her whole life running from.

Leo was right. Had always been right. Coop was going to fail her.

Coop closed his eyes. Let the darkness pull him under.

Belle had decided she was going to try. She was going to give this thing with Coop a real chance.

The kiss had changed something inside her. Or maybe it hadn't changed anything—maybe it had just revealed what was already there. That he made her feel safe.

Belle had spent so long believing safety didn't exist. That home was a lie. That trust would only lead to more pain.

But Coop—

Maybe Coop was different. Maybe she could try believing. Try trusting. Try building something real with him instead of walking away when they reached Oregon.

The thought terrified her. But it also felt like the first deep breath she'd taken in years.

Belle sat near the fire outside Evangeline and Leo's tent. The camp was quiet. Most of the men were at a meeting on the far side of the circle. Coop must be getting ready to go on watch.

Evangeline was inside the tent, tucking Sara in. Belle could hear their soft voices. Sara asking for one more story. Evangeline's gentle response.

A family. Safe and warm and together.

Maybe Belle could have that too. Maybe—

Movement caught Belle's eye.

A man emerged from the darkness beyond the wagons. Walking toward Evangeline's tent with purpose.

Belle straightened. Her hand moved instinctively toward her waist where she kept her gun strapped beneath her coat.

But then she hesitated. It was dark. Hard to see clearly. Maybe it was Leo returning from the meeting. Or one of the other men bringing a message.

The figure reached the tent entrance. Paused there.

Evangeline's voice went quiet inside.

Belle started to relax. Just someone checking on them. Nothing to—

The man backed away from the tent, pointing a revolver at Evangeline as she emerged with Sara in her arms.

Belle's heart slammed against her ribs. Her breath came short and fast.

She couldn't let this happen.

Belle's hand closed around the grip of her pistol. She drew it smoothly. Her palm was sweating but her hand was steady.

She moved across the camp. Staying low. Using the shadows. Every instinct she'd ever developed for survival screaming at her to run, to hide, to protect herself first.

But Evangeline was frozen in place. Sara was crying softly into her mother's neck.

Belle got close enough to see his face and recognition slammed into her like a fist.

She'd seen this man around Coop. Talking to him. Standing too close. Looking at Belle in a way that made her skin crawl.

He had the same dead eyes as Sarge. The same emptiness behind the smile. The same casual cruelty.

"Get away from them," Belle said. Her voice came out steady, despite the terror clawing at her throat. She raised her gun. Aimed it at his back.

The man turned slowly.

When he saw Belle, he smiled. "Well, isn't this perfect?"

His voice made Belle's stomach turn.

"My men were just delivering a message to your husband," the man continued. His gun never wavered from Evangeline and Sara. "But now I'll take this perfect opportunity that has fallen into my lap."

He flicked his gun toward Belle. "Drop it."

"Let them go," Belle said instead.

The man's smile widened. "I don't think so. Drop the gun, Mrs. Spencer. Or I'll shoot the little girl first."

Sara whimpered. Evangeline's arms tightened around her daughter.

Belle's hand started to shake. She couldn't—she couldn't let him hurt Sara. Couldn't let him hurt Evangeline.

But if she dropped the gun—

"Now," the man said.

Belle started to lower her weapon.

Then raised it fast. Aimed for his chest.

The man was faster.

His gun barked, the sound exploding through the quiet camp.

Belle's pistol flew from her hand. Pain blazed through her palm and wrist—white-hot and shocking. She cried out. Looked down.

Her hand was still attached. Still whole. But the skin across her knuckles was torn and bleeding.

"Run!" Evangeline screamed.

Belle turned. Started to run. She had to find Coop.

She made it three steps.

Something caught her ankle.

The ground slammed into her. Knocked the air from her lungs. Her chin hit first. Then her hands as she tried to catch herself.

Belle gasped. Tried to push herself up.

A boot pressed down on her back. Shoved her flat against the ground.

"Got her," a voice said above her.

Belle twisted her head. Looked up.

Another man stood over her. She recognized him too. Another one she'd seen with Coop.

They were together. Working together.

The first man—the one with the dead eyes—walked over. Still smiling that empty smile.

The man standing over Belle looked at him. "Is it done?"

"Yeah." Dead-eyes holstered his gun. "That fool Spencer isn't going to be up and walking for a good long while."

Belle's heart stopped.

Spencer. Coop.

The man grabbed Belle's arm. Yanked her to her feet. Pain shot through her shoulder.

"Start walking," dead-eyes said. He motioned with his gun toward the darkness beyond the wagons. Away from camp. Away from help. Away from Coop.

Belle's legs wouldn't move. She stared at the man. At his dead eyes and his cruel smile.

"That'll teach him to double cross us," the other man said. He twisted Belle's arm harder. Made her gasp.

The words crashed together in Belle's mind.

Coop knew these men. Was involved with these men. Had made some kind of deal with them.

And now he'd double crossed them. And they'd hurt him. Said he wouldn't be walking for a long while. Because of whatever deal he'd made with them.

Belle had trusted him. Had chosen to trust him. Had kissed him and told him her darkest secrets and believed—actually believed—that he was different. That he was safe.

But he'd been lying the whole time. Had been involved with men like these.

"Move," dead-eyes said. He shoved Belle forward.

She stumbled. Caught herself.

Evangeline was crying. Holding Sara. Being forced to walk beside Belle into the darkness.

And Coop—

Coop was hurt somewhere. Maybe dying. Because of whatever he'd done. Whatever deals he'd made with these men.

Belle had been such a fool to let herself believe. Let herself hope. Let herself think that maybe—just maybe—

there was such a thing as a safe man. A safe home. A safe future.

But there wasn't. There never had been.

Chapter Fifteen

Belle's hands were bound behind her back. The rope bit into her wrists. Cut off circulation. Made her fingers tingle and go numb.

She couldn't move them. Couldn't reach the knife hidden in her dress pocket.

Couldn't do anything.

The darkness pressed in from all sides. She didn't know how far they'd walked in the darkness. A quarter mile? A half mile? Trees loomed like black shadows. The only light came from the distant glow of the circled wagons—far enough away that screaming wouldn't help. Close enough that Belle could see the faint orange flicker through the trees.

But it might as well have been miles.

Larson—the man with the dead eyes—paced near the horses. Three other men stood nearby. One of them kept glancing toward the wagons like he wanted to run.

Evangeline sat on the ground a few feet away. Her hands were bound in front of her so she could hold Sara. The little girl was crying. Quiet, hitching sobs that shook her small body.

"Shh, sweetheart." Evangeline's voice trembled. "It's going to be alright. Shh."

But Sara wouldn't stop.

Belle couldn't feel anything except the pounding of her heart and the sick, hollow fear in her stomach.

She'd failed. Had tried to protect them and failed.

One of the men—the one who kept glancing at the wagons—moved closer to Larson. "I never signed up for kidnapping women." His voice was tight. Scared. "I don't wanna be a part of this anymore."

Larson stopped pacing. Turned to face him. The firelight from the distant camp caught the edge of his face. Made his smile look like a skull.

"It's too late for that." Larson's voice was calm. "What's done is done."

"But—"

"I've had my ears to the ground since the beginning of this journey." Larson took a step closer to the nervous man. "I know that Leo Spencer is sitting on a wagon full of gold. It was just luck that his brother came to me for a loan."

Gold. Leo's gold.

Coop had borrowed money from this man. Had gotten involved with him. Had made deals with him.

Belle had wondered where Coop's sudden windfall had come from. She'd never asked. Would he have told her the truth if she had? She felt like she didn't know him at all.

"I aim to take control of all that gold," Larson continued. "Make tracks down to California. Start a new life."

The nervous man shifted on his feet. "Gold's pretty heavy. How are you gonna get away with—"

Larson's fist connected with the man's jaw. Fast. Brutal. The crack echoed through the darkness.

The man went down hard. Didn't get back up.

Sara's crying grew louder.

"Make her be quiet," Larson said. He didn't raise his voice. Didn't need to. The threat was clear.

"I'm trying," Evangeline whispered. She rocked Sara. Pressed her daughter's face against her shoulder. "Shh, baby. Please. Please be quiet."

But Sara was beyond soothing. Beyond comfort. She was a little girl who'd been ripped from her bed and dragged into the dark by men with guns.

Just like Belle had been.

Larson stalked toward them. His boots crunched on the forest floor.

He stopped in front of Evangeline. Leaned down. Got right in her face.

"Make the girl be quiet," he said. His voice dropped low. Dangerous. "Or I'll do it."

Belle's heart stopped. Her breath caught in her throat.

She knew what that meant. Knew what men like Larson did to little girls who wouldn't be quiet.

Evangeline knew, too. Her face went white. Her arms tightened around Sara so hard the little girl whimpered.

Belle wanted to move. Wanted to do something. Wanted to grab her knife and—

But she was frozen.

One of the other men—not the one Larson had hit—

walked past Belle. His boot kicked against hers as he went by. Not hard. Just enough to make her flinch.

She heard him laugh. "Maybe Larson will let us rough her up a bit. Have a little fun." Too quiet for Larson to hear. But Belle heard. "I heard she used to be a saloon girl. Bet she knows how to—"

Belle started shaking. She felt like she might fly apart.

She'd tried to escape, but there was no escaping the life she'd been sold into.

Her vision blurred. The darkness seemed to press closer. Suffocating.

She couldn't breathe. Couldn't think.

Belle was eight years old again. Standing in that tiny dugout. Tasting blood in her mouth. Learning that home wasn't safe. That the people who were supposed to love you could hurt you. That when things spun out of control, violence followed.

She was fourteen again. Running from the brothel. Being dragged back. Beaten. Locked in a room. Told she'd never be free. Never be safe. Never be anything more than what they had made her.

Or weeks ago, she'd been watching Sarge kill her friend. Watching Pretty die. Knowing it could be her. Would be her, eventually.

And now she was here. In the darkness. With Evangeline and Sara. With men who wanted to hurt them. Use them. Destroy them.

Belle's teeth chattered. Her breath came in short, sharp gasps that didn't bring enough air.

She couldn't hear anything except the roaring in her ears and Sara's quiet sobs and the men's low laughter and Larson's calm, deadly voice saying something about moving out at first light.

No one was coming. No one knew where they were. Coop was hurt—maybe dead—back at camp. Leo was still out searching for Sarge. The other men were at the meeting.

By the time anyone realized they were missing, it would be too late.

Belle had tried so hard. Had fought so hard. Had run and struggled and clawed her way toward something that looked like freedom.

But there was no freedom.

There was only this. The darkness. The rope. The men with their cruel smiles and their plans to use her.

Everything Belle had feared was coming true.

And she was powerless to stop it.

Every step was agony.

Coop's ribs screamed with each breath. His left eye was swollen nearly shut. Blood dripped from the gash above his eyebrow.

He couldn't stand upright. Could barely walk. Had to half-crawl, half-stumble through the darkness toward the orange glow of the circled wagons.

Coop needed to talk to Leo. He was going to come clean, confess to everything. No matter what Belle thought of him, he had to make sure she was protected. It was the only thing he could be thankful for in this moment—that Belle was safe in camp.

Coop stumbled into the firelight. Fell to his knees.

Voices. Movement. People running.

"Coop!" Leo's voice. Sharp. Urgent.

Coop tried to stand. Couldn't. His ribs wouldn't let him.

Hands grabbed him. Held him up. Leo's face swam into view. Then Owen's. Rachel was there, too.

Collin pushed forward. "What happened?"

Coop shook his head. "Collin—can you check on Belle? I wanna make sure Belle is okay."

Collin's eyes widened, but he turned. Ran toward the Spencer wagon.

Coop swallowed every bit of pride. Looked at Leo. "I need money."

"Where's the doc?" Leo called over his shoulder. Not listening.

"Leo—" Coop tried again.

"What happened? Who did this?"

Coop spat blood. "Larson. His men. They were sending a message."

Coop's ears were ringing. His vision kept blurring.

Movement in the darkness. Someone stumbling toward them.

Matt—one of the cowboys—emerged from between the wagons. His hand pressed to his head. A nasty bump visible even in the firelight. He swayed on his feet.

"Leo. I need you."

Leo didn't let go of his hold on Coop. If he did, Coop would probably flop to the ground.

Owen caught Matt before he fell. Helped him to the ground.

"Matt!" Lily's voice rang out as she ran toward them, skirts gathered in her hands. She dropped to her knees beside her husband, hands hovering over the wound on his head. "You're bleeding—"

"I'm alright," Matt said, though his words slurred. He caught her hand. "Two men took Evangeline and Sara and Belle out of camp—"

Lily's face went white.

"I tried to stop them. Someone hit me from behind. Knocked me out cold."

Larson took Belle.

Larson. And another man.

Coop went stiff.

Leo was looking at him. Not understanding yet.

"We gotta go after them," Coop said. "He will hurt them."

"What do you know of Larson?"

Running footsteps. Collin sprinting back to the group.

"Did you do this?" Then Leo realized. Coop could see the moment it clicked.

Leo let go.

Coop fell back to his knees. Pain exploded through his ribs.

"Are you mixed up with him?" Leo's voice rose. "Are you the reason my wife was just kidnapped from camp?"

"I didn't—" Coop tasted blood again. "I didn't know he would—"

"Why didn't you ask me for what you needed?"

The question hung in the air.

Something broke inside Coop.

Leo stared at him.

Jason appeared. Took one look at Coop and came straight toward him.

Leo paced away. His hand rubbed the back of his neck. He muttered to Collin. "We have to go after them. Right now."

Coop tried to stand up.

"Whoa, whoa, whoa." Jason pressed him back down. "Busted rib. Maybe two. You need to lie down."

"You better make it fast because I'm going after my wife."

"You're not going anywhere. You can't even walk."

Leo came back. "Move him over here. Away from the others."

Owen and Jason helped Coop to his feet. Half-carried him to the edge of the circle.

Leo's face was hard. "How many men does Larson have?"

Coop tried to focus through the pain. "At least three. Maybe more. They're armed."

"Where would he take them?"

"I don't know."

The world tilted. Went gray at the edges.

He swayed. Jason caught him.

"He cannot ride out with you guys," Jason said to Leo. "Look at him."

Coop tried to push to his feet. Couldn't.

"If you go off half-cocked—" Leo crossed the space between them. Got right in Coop's face. "If you rush out into those woods without a plan, you're going to get my wife killed."

Leo turned away. Started giving orders.

While Coop sat there. Jason bandaging him. Coop's head

pounding so hard he couldn't think straight. Couldn't physically stand up.

He watched Leo instructing Collin and the other men. People jumping into action. Preparing to ride out.

Belle was out there in the darkness. Terrified. And alone with men who would hurt her.

Because of him.

I will never forgive you. The words echoed in Coop's chest. In the hollow place where his hope used to be.

He'd destroyed everything.

Chapter Sixteen

Coop moved around the outside of the circled wagons, keeping to the shadows. Each step sent fire through his ribs.

The cowboy camp was empty. The men were with Leo—things had been set in motion. Men riding out of camp in pairs. Leo already out there somewhere.

After Doc had patched Coop up and left him by the fire, Doc went to help search, too. But Coop couldn't just sit there and do nothing.

He reached his horse. Grabbed the saddle from the ground with shaking hands. Every movement was agony. He had to stop twice, breathe through the pain, before he could lift the saddle onto Scout's back.

His hands fumbled with the cinch. Pulled it tight.

"I saw you sneak out of camp."

Coop turned. Collin stood a few feet away.

"Don't try to stop me," Coop said.

"I'm not." Collin came up beside him. Grabbed his own

rifle. "But you're barely standing. You're gonna get yourself killed."

"As long as the women are safe, I don't care."

The words came out before Coop could stop them. And they were true.

Collin was quiet for a moment. Then: "Are you coming or not?"

Movement behind them. Matt jogging toward the horses from camp. He nodded at the two of them. "I'm with you."

Collin had to help Coop into the saddle. The pain nearly made him black out. But once he was up, once he had the reins in his hands, Coop felt steadier.

They rode into the woods the opposite direction from where the others had gone. Three men on horseback. Moving as quietly as they could.

The trail wasn't hard to follow. Broken branches. Trampled snow. Boot prints.

Coop moved on instinct. Tried to remember everything August had taught him about tracking. August had been patient with him over these past weeks—showing Coop how sound and scent could tell a story when sight failed. How to read the forest through touch and memory. It was strange learning from a blind man how to see more clearly, but August had found his own way of navigating the wilderness. Had found his purpose again.

Coop's head pounded. His vision swam. But he kept moving.

Voices carried through the darkness. Low. Arguing.

Collin held up a hand.

They dismounted. Moved slower. Careful not to make noise. Using trees for cover.

Coop could see them now.

Belle sat on the ground. Hands bound behind her. Evangeline held Sara.

Larson paced near the horses.

One man sat on the ground with his hand pressed over one eye. Seth was smoking his pipe. Another man stood near Seth.

Rage burned hot in Coop's chest. He raised his rifle. Sighted down the barrel. His hands shook.

Collin touched his shoulder. Mouthed, *wait*.

But Coop couldn't wait.

He burst out of the trees. Collin and Matt right behind him.

"Don't move!"

Everything happened at once.

One of Larson's men went for his gun. Collin fired. The man went down.

The man sitting on the ground raised his hands. "Don't shoot! I don't wanna be a part of this!"

The third man bolted into the woods. Matt chased after another fellow. Both disappeared into the darkness.

And Larson—

Larson moved faster than Coop expected. Grabbed Sara right out of Evangeline's arms. The little girl screamed.

"Larson!" Coop swung his rifle toward the man. But Larson was already backing away. Using Sara as a shield.

"Come any closer and I'll hurt the girl," Larson said.

Coop's hands shook on the rifle. He couldn't take the shot.

"Let her go," Coop said.

Larson smiled. Then turned and ran into the woods.

Sara's screams faded into the darkness.

Evangeline sobbed. Tried to struggle to her feet. To go after him.

Collin moved to Evangeline. The man he'd shot lay unmoving on the ground.

Coop stumbled toward Belle. Each step sent fire through his ribs.

He dropped to his knees in front of her. Pulled out his knife with shaking hands.

"I've got you," he said. "You're safe now."

He cut the ropes binding her wrists.

Collin cut Evangeline's bonds. She immediately tried to run after Sara. Collin caught her. Held her back.

"We'll find her," Collin said.

But Evangeline was screaming. Sobbing.

Coop turned back to Belle. Reached for her.

She flinched away.

Turned her face from him. Wouldn't meet his eyes.

The rejection hit harder than any punch Larson's men had landed.

"Belle—"

She pulled away. Stood up on shaking legs. Moved toward Evangeline.

Away from Coop.

Thunder of hoofbeats. More horses crashing through the woods.

Leo burst into the clearing. Owen right behind him. More men following.

Leo read the scene in an instant. The dead man. The one sitting on the ground with hands raised. Evangeline sobbing. Belle standing apart, shaking.

And Sara gone.

Leo went to Evangeline. Touched her wrist.

"Where's Sara?"

"Larson took her." Collin spoke. "Matt chased after another fellow."

Leo closed his eyes. His jaw clenched.

Coop pushed to his feet. Staggered to the man still sitting on the ground. Grabbed him by the front of his shirt and hauled him up. "Where did he go? Where would Larson take her?"

The man's eyes went wide. "I don't know! I didn't want any part of this!"

"You were with him!" Coop shook him. Pain shot through his ribs. "Where would he go?"

"You know as much as I do." The man twisted in Coop's grip. "I swear I don't know."

Larson wasn't one to tell his plans. He'd never told Coop who he wanted to collect from until he'd assigned him the job. This guy was probably telling the truth. He was someone just like Coop—mixed up in a terrible situation.

"Coop." Leo's voice cut through. "Let him go."

Coop released the man. Turned to meet Leo's icy stare. "You told me not to come out here, but I couldn't just sit there—"

Leo's voice was flat. Cold. "You didn't think, Coop. You never do. And now Larson has my daughter. If you just would've waited, we could have gotten everyone out safely."

Leo took a step closer. Looked Coop straight in the eye. "You've made this so much worse."

Leo turned away. As if he couldn't waste any more time

on his brother. He moved to talk to Collin. Sent two men riding out into the dark.

Coop looked at Belle. She still wouldn't face him. Her arms were wrapped around her shaking body.

He'd done this.

He'd broken everything. Again.

And this time, the pieces couldn't be put back together.

Belle couldn't stop trembling.

The ropes were gone, but Belle could still feel them. The bite of rough hemp against her wrists. The numbness in her fingers. The helplessness.

Maddie had met her and Coop at the edge of camp when Matt had escorted them back. Coop was sitting by the fire now, staring into the flames. Maddie finished putting salve on a scrape on Belle's jaw.

"You're safe now," Maddie murmured.

But Belle didn't feel safe.

Maddie straightened. "I need to go check on the kids. I'll come back in just a few minutes."

She passed Coop on her way. "You don't move. You're going to injure yourself worse."

Belle was aware of Coop watching her. She couldn't look at him. But he had come.

And for one moment, she had felt relief so intense it hurt.

She had wanted to run to him. Wanted to feel his arms around her, hear him say it was going to be all right.

In that moment, she had realized something.

She had fallen for him.

Somewhere between the river and the fire and the kiss freely given, Belle had fallen for Coop Spencer.

Coop got up from the fire. Winced. It was obvious he was badly hurt. That every movement caused him pain. Yet he still hadn't listened to Maddie.

He moved toward her.

"I am so sorry," he said.

Belle couldn't look up. If she did, she might break.

"I made a mistake. I thought I could pay him back for the loan I took, but I was wrong. And you paid the price."

His words opened up the hollowness inside her even more.

She had to find a way to make him understand.

"I see now that I can't depend on you," Belle said.

He flinched. Like the words had hit him.

She tried to soften them. "I can't depend on anyone. I can't be in a situation where someone else makes decisions for me. I can't trust—" Her voice broke.

"So that's it?" His voice was hollow. "There's no chance for us?"

Belle couldn't answer.

Movement at the edge of camp.

Leo escorted Evangeline into the clearing. She was wrapped in a blanket. Her face streaked with tears. Her shoulders slumped. Like she was grieving. Like somebody had died.

Leo shot one disgusted look at Coop, then led Evangeline to meet Maddie several yards away.

Belle felt a beat of compassion for Coop. Leo had been hard on him. Coop staring after Leo now.

It hurt her to see him hurting. She knew how desperately he wanted his brother's approval. The whole situation was terrible.

Evangeline had lost Sara, despite being married to Leo. Being married to someone hadn't protected her from this situation.

Belle wished she could say something to Coop. But there was nothing left to say between them. She tucked her face into the blanket wrapped around her shoulders. Closed her eyes. Heard Coop walk away.

If this was for the best, why did it feel like her heart was breaking?

Belle opened her eyes. Looked toward the wagons.

Through a gap between two canvas covers, she could see the herd of cattle. Some of those animals were supposed to be her future. She'd done everything she could to believe in and plan for that future—and look what'd happened.

She'd been grabbed by an evil man.

Sara was still in danger.

There was no hope for the shining future Coop had painted for her.

The stamp of a horse nearby made her jump. A man's voice carried across camp. Wind rustled through the trees.

Sarge was still out there. Somewhere. He'd tracked her this far, taken a shot and nearly hit her. He wouldn't stop.

She wasn't safe. She never had been.

Belle pushed to her feet. The blanket fell from her shoulders. She moved to the tent and ducked inside, started gathering her belongings.

She didn't have much. A spare dress. It didn't really belong to her, but what use did Coop have for it? She'd leave behind the men's clothing Stella had loaned her. She shouldn't take the shawl. But she'd need it for warmth.

That was it. Everything she owned in the world fit in a small bundle.

Belle rolled the dress tight.

The gun belt lay on top of Coop's bedroll. The revolver Coop had taught her to shoot.

Belle stared at it.

It hadn't done her any good. She'd tried to use it to protect Evangeline and Sara. And Larson had shot it right out of her hand.

It wasn't hers anyway. It was Coop's.

Belle left it there.

She would go in the morning. Sneak away from camp and run. Even if it didn't bring Sara back, if Belle left, then maybe Sarge would give chase. Leave the wagon train, and the Spencer family, alone.

Her hand went to the silver ring on her finger.

She needed to leave everything that reminded her of Coop behind.

Chapter Seventeen

Belle hadn't slept one wink. She'd lain in the tent all night, listening. Hoping that there'd be noise of men coming into camp, jubilant voices. Praying for Sara to be returned.

But there'd only been terrible silence. A handful of whispers.

When she couldn't stand to lie in bed any longer, she sat up.

She pushed out of the tent, the bundle of her clothing in one hand. The camp was mostly quiet, the sky just beginning to lighten on the eastern horizon. A low fire burned near the Spencer wagon, someone tending it.

Maddie.

The woman motioned Belle to join her at the campfire. Belle almost refused, almost turned and walked out of camp.

But Maddie had been the first one to notice Belle when she'd been sneaking around the camp, stealing to survive. She'd been a friend before Belle had known she needed one.

The least she could do was say goodbye.

Maddie looked up as Belle approached. Her eyes were kind and concerned.

"Couldn't sleep? Here, sit down."

Belle nodded as she sat on a log near the fire—just for a minute. Wrapped her arms around herself. The morning air was cold and sharp. How had Sara fared out there without a blanket to keep her warm? Was she all right?

"How are you feeling?" Maddie asked as she stirred something savory in a pot over the fire. Soup? The smell made Belle's stomach clench.

"I—don't know." She ached all over, but the worst pain was in her heart.

Her stomach growled, the sound loud in the quiet.

Maddie smiled gently. "When did you eat last?"

"I don't remember." What did food matter at a time like this?

Maddie ladled broth into a tin cup and circled the fire to hand it to Belle. "You need to eat. It'll help."

Belle took the cup. Her wedding ring clinked against the metal of the cup. She hadn't been able to take it off after all. Warmth seeped into her hands, but her insides still felt frozen. What would eating help? It wouldn't help find Sara.

She should get up and leave, do what she'd decided to do last night. But her entire body felt weighted down. And she was hungry.

When she sipped, the broth was hot and savory.

"How's Coop?" Maddie asked quietly. "Did he sleep at all?"

Belle's throat tightened. "I don't know."

Maddie's eyebrows rose. "He didn't come to the tent?"

Belle shook her head. Stared into her cup.

"That man better not have gone back out looking for Sara," Maddie muttered as she gave the pot another stir. "He has a good heart." Her voice turned soft and thoughtful. "But that impulsiveness can get him into trouble. I know he only wanted to rescue you and Evangeline and Sara last night. Everyone's been on edge since—"

Since Sarge.

Belle didn't say anything. Couldn't.

"He'll make a good father for your children," Maddie continued. "I can see that he's settled down just since the two of you were married. He's made better choices. He's trying to do the right thing. Growing up." She glanced up at Belle directly. "He'll make a good husband."

The words deepened the ache in Belle's chest. She shook her head, unable to meet Maddie's eyes.

"What is it?" Maddie asked gently.

The lingering taste in Belle's mouth soured. She took a shaky breath. "Our marriage. It's not real."

"What do you mean?" Maddie's voice held genuine confusion. "I was one of the witnesses when Hollis hitched you."

"We made an agreement." Belle's voice came out flat. "Once we reach Oregon, we'll have it annulled. Neither one of us wanted this marriage."

Maddie was quiet for a long moment. Then she said softly, "I don't know if that's true. Coop has been infatuated with you from the start."

Belle's chest tightened. She thought about the kiss by the fire. About Coop holding her through the night. About the way he looked at her.

Maybe Maddie was right. Maybe Coop did want more. But Belle couldn't give it to him.

"He might make a good husband," Belle said quietly. "But I would never be able to be a good wife."

The words hung in the air. They felt so final.

"Why do you say that?" Maddie asked.

Belle stared into the fire and watched the flames dance. "I look at you and Doc. Rachel and Owen. The way you trust him. The way she submits to him." She shook her head. "I don't have it in me to do that."

Maddie stirred the broth. Quiet. Giving Belle space to continue.

"My uncle—" Belle's voice cracked. She had to stop. Had to breathe. "He was a friend of the family. He was supposed to protect me after my pa died. But instead he—he sold me."

She swallowed hard.

"Those parts of me were taken away," Belle whispered. "I can't... trust. I can't submit. I never should've made the vows I did."

Maddie's hand reached out and covered Belle's.

"I'm so sorry," Maddie said. "That should never have happened to you."

They sat in silence for a moment. The fire crackling. The camp slowly waking around them.

Finally, Maddie spoke. "Do you know the story of Job from the Bible?"

Belle shook her head.

"Job was a man who had everything taken from him," Maddie said. "His children. His wealth. His health. Everything was stripped away. His friends told him it must be because he'd done something wrong. That God was punishing him."

Belle listened. Watched Maddie's face in the firelight.

"But Job chose to trust God anyway," Maddie continued. "Even when he didn't understand. Even when everything hurt. He said, 'Though He slay me, yet will I trust in Him.' Because Job knew something important."

"What?" Belle's voice was barely a whisper.

"That God is trustworthy. The only One who is truly, completely trustworthy. The only One who will never abandon us. Never betray us. Never use us for His own gain."

The words settled into Belle's chest. She wanted to believe so badly.

"Jason and I—we didn't see eye to eye at first," Maddie said. A small smile touched her lips as her eyes went distant. "We had a lot of arguments. It took a while for me to learn to trust him."

Belle thought about Coop. About how afraid she'd been at first. How she'd been so sure he was dangerous.

"But I learned something," Maddie said. "Submitting to a husband—to a godly husband—isn't being trapped with a man who would hurt you or punish you. It's choosing to trust someone who loves you. Who would die for you. The way Christ died for us."

Belle's breath caught. Rachel had told her the same thing, hadn't she? But Belle hadn't been able to see it.

"God is a good God," Maddie said. "He sent His son to earth to bring His people freedom. Not to trap them. Jesus said, 'If the Son sets you free, you will be free indeed.' True freedom isn't about being alone. It's about surrendering to the One who loves you perfectly."

The truth of it hit Belle like a wave.

Freedom. Not control.

Surrender. Not slavery.

Belle thought about everything that had happened since she'd escaped Virgil and the brothel. She'd happened onto *this* wagon train and stowed away in Maddie's wagon. She'd met Maddie. Alex and Paul.

Coop.

Rob had protected her, injuring himself in the process.

Alice had taught her how to cook.

Hollis had agreed to protect her.

Coop provided that tent. New clothes.

Taught her to ride, to shoot.

Dove into the river after her. Kept her warm even when it meant his own suffering. Held her through the night. Listened to her darkest stories. Cared for her.

Cared about her?

All of it. Every bit of it. Leading her here. To this moment. To this truth.

She wasn't trapped anymore.

Sarge might be out there, still hunting her. But Belle wasn't the same terrified girl who'd fled the brothel.

She wasn't powerless. Wasn't friendless or helpless.

God had brought her through it all. Had protected her. Had kept her alive when she should have died a dozen times over.

God had brought her to the wagon train when she was desperate and alone in the wilderness. Had given her people to stand beside her. To teach her. To care for her.

God hadn't abandoned her or left her to suffer alone.

And if God was trustworthy—if God truly loved her the way Maddie said—then maybe Belle could trust Him. Could surrender to Him and let go of the way she'd tried to control her life, her future.

Belle felt something rise inside her chest. Something that had been locked tight for so long.

Peace. Quiet and warm and unexpected.

"Thank you," Belle whispered. Tears stung her eyes. "Thank you for being my friend."

Maddie smiled. Then she pulled Belle into a hug.

Belle let herself be held. Let the tears come. Let herself feel—really feel—for the first time in years.

She wasn't trapped. She was free.

Free to choose. Free to trust. Free to surrender to the God who loved her.

Maddie pulled back. Dabbed a tear from Belle's cheek with her sleeve. "I need to go check on my kids. Make sure they're still asleep." She smiled. "You finish your soup."

Belle nodded. Couldn't speak past the emotion in her throat.

She closed her eyes. Let the morning air wash over her. Let the peace settle deeper.

God, I don't know how to do this. Don't know how to trust. But I want to. I want to be free. Really free. So I'm choosing to trust You. To surrender to You. To let You lead me wherever You want me to go.

The prayer felt awkward. Unfamiliar. But also—right.

Belle opened her eyes as the sun began to rise over the mountains, painting the sky in shades of pink and gold.

Nearby, urgent voices drew her attention.

Belle turned toward Leo and Evangeline's tent.

Evangeline had collapsed into Leo's arms, sobbing.

Leo hadn't wanted to come back to the company.

He'd argued with Owen, wasting precious moments. Insisted he should keep searching. Sara was out there. His daughter was out there in the cold with a dangerous man.

But Owen had been firm. "You need to check on Evangeline. She needs you."

Evangeline.

His wife. Who'd also been taken. Who must have been terrified. Who was probably falling apart while Leo was out in the woods chasing shadows.

So Leo had returned, even though every instinct screamed at him to keep going.

The camp came into view. Wagons circled. Fires burning low. People moving quietly in the early morning light.

Snow had started falling again. Fine, fluffy flakes that weren't obscuring much yet. But they would. Before long, the tracks would be covered over.

And Sara would be even harder to find.

Leo dismounted. His legs were stiff and sore. He'd been in the saddle all night without sleep.

The wilderness was too big. A man on horseback could disappear anywhere.

Leo's chest felt tight. Hollow. How would he find Sara when Larson could be hiding anywhere?

Leo walked toward his wagon and the fire burning nearby.

Evangeline was scrambling out of their tent. Tears streaked her cheeks, and when she caught sight of him, her face crumpled.

And Leo saw it. The devastation. The terror. The grief.

She swayed toward him.

Leo closed the distance, grabbed her and pulled her against his chest.

And Evangeline broke.

She sobbed. Her whole body shaking. Her hands clutching Leo's coat like she was drowning and he was the only solid thing left.

Leo held her. Tucked his head down against hers. Felt her tears soak into his shirt. Blinked back tears of his own. The storm lasted a long time.

Finally, Evangeline pushed away. She sniffled, trying to catch her breath.

Leo let her go reluctantly.

He took his hat off. Ran his hand through his hair. Tried to think.

"I'm going to grab something to eat and go back out there," Leo said. "I wish I had August and his tracking skills. We would have already found her."

Evangeline opened her mouth. Closed it. Couldn't seem to find words.

She turned her head slightly toward the fire. The light illuminated a scrape on her jaw, dark against her pale skin. A bruise forming.

Evangeline had been hurt.

He'd been so focused on Sara that he'd barely thought about what his wife had been through.

"How are you?" Leo stepped closer, cupped her jaw gently in his hand. "Are you hurt? Did they—"

Evangeline shook her head.

Hot anger surged through him.

"This is all Coop's fault," Leo said. "He made some deal with Larson that went bad. I can't believe he would—"

Evangeline shook her head, dislodging his hand.

"What?" Leo demanded.

"Out in the woods—" Evangeline's hoarse voice was barely a whisper. "Larson said he wants the gold. The gold Father left behind."

Leo went still, pulse pounding in his head. "What?"

"He wants the gold," Evangeline repeated. "That's what he said. That he'd had his ears to the ground since the beginning. That he was waiting for the right opportunity to take it from us. From me."

Leo stared at her. His exhausted mind tried to process what she was telling him.

The gold. Not Coop's debt.

"But—" Leo shook his head. "Coop admitted he made a deal with Larson. That he borrowed money."

"I have the words straight from Larson's mouth." Evangeline paused. Took a shaky breath. "And a man's been sneaking around our campsite. Watching from behind a wagon, staying in the shadows. I—I started carrying a derringer. Little good it did."

"What?" Leo's voice rose. "Why didn't you tell me?"

Evangeline looked away. "You've been so busy with the

company. So frustrated over your brother. I didn't want to add to your troubles."

He'd been impatient and distant.

She didn't have to say the words. He knew them, deep in his heart. Owen had told him something was bothering Evangeline. And Leo had been too stubborn, too focused on fixing Coop's mess to pay attention.

He cupped her elbow in his hand. Swallowed against the hot knot in his throat.

"You're my wife," Leo said. "You should be able to come to me about anything. Anything, Evangeline. I'm sorry if I made you feel otherwise."

New tears gathered in her eyes and she ducked her head, but didn't move away.

He hadn't been paying attention to what truly mattered. His wife. His daughter. His family.

And now Sara was gone. And it was Leo's fault as much as anyone's.

"If Coop would have fallen in line months ago," Leo's voice came out hard, "none of this would have happened."

"That's not true."

The voice came from behind Leo, quiet but firm.

Leo turned. Belle stood at the edge of their fire. He hadn't heard her approach.

Her eyes blazed, her chin set with determination.

"Coop has always wanted to be what you want him to be," Belle said. "But he's always found it impossible. He's broken over what happened." She paused. "He's a good man."

Leo started to interrupt. But Belle kept going.

"He'll never be like you," Belle said. "But that doesn't mean he's a bad person. He thinks differently than you. He wants different things out of life than you. But he still loves you deeply." Her voice cracked. "And he needs his big brother."

Leo had never heard her speak so many words. He stood stunned, staring at this woman who'd married his brother. A woman he barely knew.

Evangeline's hand slipped into his, her fingers cold and trembling. She leaned close to whisper in his ear. "Remember the story of the prodigal son?"

The prodigal son.

The words jogged loose a memory of Ma reading the Bible after supper. Reading the story of a younger son who took his inheritance and squandered it. Who came home broken. Who was welcomed back by his father with open arms.

And the older son who'd stayed, who'd been faithful, who'd done everything right.

And who'd been angry when his father celebrated the younger son's return.

Leo's breath caught.

It hit him with terrible clarity. He could be a mirror image of the older brother from that Bible story.

He'd resented Coop for being reckless, for making mistakes and not having to carry the weight Leo carried.

Leo had told himself it was about keeping Coop safe. About protecting him from his own bad choices.

But it wasn't. Not really.

It was about Leo's own pain. His resentment that Coop got to be the prodigal while Leo had to be the responsible one.

And Leo had let that resentment poison their relationship.

But the father in that story—the father loved both sons. Welcomed both of them. Celebrated both of them.

Because they both belonged.

And God—God loved both Leo and Coop.

Leo's throat tightened, but he made himself look at Belle. This woman who'd seen something in Coop worth defending.

"Thank you," Leo said. "For setting me straight. I'm glad he's got a wife like you to take care of him."

Belle looked stricken for a flicker of a second before her expression went carefully blank. Then she slipped away.

Leo turned back to Evangeline. She watched him, emotion written across her expressive features. She'd been telling him for weeks that he needed to make things right with Coop. Before today, he just hadn't been able to see.

He leaned down to kiss her cheek. Tasted salt.

"I've got to go find our daughter," Leo said quietly.

Evangeline nodded. "Please be careful."

Leo grabbed his coat. Started toward the horses.

He had a daughter to find. A brother to reconcile with. A family to put back together.

And this time, he'd do it right.

The morning was cold and gray. Snow still falling, now in lazy drifts.

Coop tightened the cinch on his saddle even though his

ribs protested. Every movement hurt. His face was a mess of bruises and cuts. His left eye still swollen.

But he couldn't stay in camp. Couldn't sit still, *rest*, while Sara was out there.

He caught movement in his peripheral vision. Someone approaching the horses. He recognized the dark hair beneath the hat, his brother's gait.

Leo. He must be leading his horse by the reins.

Coop kept his head down. Braced himself for another explosion.

Footsteps crunched in the snow, getting closer.

Coop focused on the saddle. On breathing. On anything except his brother.

But then Leo stopped only a few feet away from Coop. Stood silent, obviously waiting.

Coop didn't want another fight. Didn't have the energy for it. But his brother wasn't going away. He looked up, braced for another tongue-lashing.

"Would you ride with me?"

Surprised, Coop froze, his hands going still on the saddle.

"I could use your eyes," Leo continued.

Coop met Leo's stare over the back of his horse.

Leo's expression was drawn and tired. But not angry.

Coop swallowed hard. Was this an olive branch? Or just false hope? "All right."

Coop pulled himself into the saddle. Winced as his ribs screamed, but bit down on the pain.

Leo swung up onto his horse. "I thought we'd go back to where you and Collin and Matt found Larson with the women. Start fresh. Maybe in the daylight, we'll see something we missed."

Coop nodded again. Couldn't speak past the pain shooting through his bones.

They rode out side by side.

It was the first time they'd spent any measure of time together without arguing.

In the woods, Coop dismounted near the tree where Belle had been tied. He could still see the haunted expression on her face when he'd come to cut her free. *I can't let myself depend on anyone.*

"Belle seemed sure Larson went west," Coop said. His voice came out rough.

Leo nodded. Coop painfully mounted back up.

At first, the tracks were almost impossible to follow. Dozens of horses had been through here last night as Leo had called men to help find Sara. The ground was churned up. But as they ranged out farther from Larson's makeshift camp, the signs got clearer.

Broken branches. Crushed snow, like someone had moved in a hurry.

Coop whistled, short and sharp.

Leo looked over, reined in his horse to join Coop.

Coop pointed. "Someone came through here moving fast."

Leo studied the ground. "Let's go."

They dismounted and moved forward on foot, leading their horses as they followed the trail of broken branches and disturbed snow.

And then Leo spoke. "Your wife told me off back at camp."

Coop's head snapped up. "What?"

"She thinks I've been too hard on you all these years."

Belle had defended him? To Leo? Why would she?

"I think maybe she's right," Leo said quietly.

Coop couldn't believe what his brother was saying. Was this a fever dream because of the pain? He tried to focus.

"Just before Ma died—" Had Leo ever taken this tone with Coop before? Patient and a little emotional? "She made me promise to take care of Alice and you boys. And I wasn't ready for that kind of responsibility."

When Coop glanced over, Leo was staring straight ahead, jaw tight.

"I barely had any knowledge of how the world worked. Didn't know anything about raising you and Collin. And I—I think I handled it wrong."

Coop's throat tightened.

"After what happened in New Jersey—" Leo stopped walking. Turned to face Coop. "I should've come to find you first. Shouldn't have blamed you immediately. Should've asked what happened. Should've been on your side."

Coop's eyes burned. He looked away.

"I shouldn't have been drinking that night," Coop said. "And I should have come and got help when Tann and Oliver refused to leave." His voice cracked. "Even if I wasn't working in the mill that night, what happened was still my fault."

They were close enough now that Leo reached out and put his hand on Coop's shoulder.

"I know they were your friends," Leo said quietly. "And you never would have meant for something like that to happen."

Coop swallowed hard. "I've done a lot of things I shouldn't. Been in a lot of places I shouldn't. There's a reason Belle doesn't want to stay married to me. I'm not the kind of man I should be." He met Leo's eyes. "I'm not like you."

Leo's hand tightened on Coop's shoulder. "Evangeline reminded me of the Bible story of the prodigal son. Ma told it to us, once. Do you remember?"

Coop had to think hard through the pounding in his head. How long ago had that been? Years. "I think so."

"I hadn't thought about how that story fit the two of us. Two brothers. I never should've let myself resent you," Leo said softly. "I've asked God to forgive me, and I'll ask you, too. But I really want to make sure you know that it doesn't matter how far you've strayed, God's been waiting for you to come back to Him, just like the little brother in that parable. All you have to do is take the first step."

God wasn't like Leo, waiting to punish him? He was a father who loved his son and wanted him home?

"I wish it was true," Coop whispered.

"It is," Leo said.

They started walking again, following the trail.

Coop took a deep breath. Let it out slowly. Felt something settle inside him. Something that had been twisted and wrong for so long.

He was God's son. Valued. Wanted. Even though he was imperfect. Even though he'd made plenty of mistakes. The knowledge settled deep, filled him with warmth and peace.

He looked at Leo.

"Thank you," Coop said. "I'm sorry, too."

"I told Belle I was glad you've got a wife like her."

The words hit hard, pain worse than the beating Coop had taken. He ran one hand down his face beneath his hat.

"What?" Leo pressed.

Coop confessed to all of it. He had no pride left. He finished with, "I promised her an annulment when we reach Oregon. After everything she's been through, I won't go back on my word."

"And she won't change her mind?" It had been a very long time since he'd heard gentleness in Leo's voice like he did now.

"Naw." Coop's throat felt raw. "She told me as much." *I can't let myself depend on anyone.*

Leaves rustled beneath Leo's feet as they continued on. "I've been watching the two of you, closer than I should've with—with everything. She watches you—"

"Because she's scared of me."

Leo shook his head. "She watches you like she can't quite believe you're real. She cares about you. Anybody with eyes can see it. Maybe she's scared of how she feels about you."

The words were a shock of hope to Coop's system. Hope that he quickly squashed.

All this time, he'd told himself—promised Belle—that he was going to be a new man. She wanted the annulment. He had to keep his word.

Leo glanced at him again. "I won't give up hope that she'll come around. There's still a few days left."

Emotion swamped Coop. Even through all the trouble he'd caused, he'd gotten his brother back. Maybe this peace between them wouldn't last, but right now, Coop was grateful.

Coop looked back at the trail. At the broken branches and crushed snow.

Then he saw it. A hoof print. Clear in the fresh snow. Leading deeper into the woods.

"There." Coop pointed.

Leo started walking faster.

A sound. Quiet. Like a whimper.

Both brothers froze. Looked at each other.

Leo jerked his head toward the noise. Tossed his horse's reins over a low branch.

Coop did the same. Drew his gun. Moved silently through the trees.

Leo pointed left. Coop nodded. Went right.

They moved in sync, maybe for the first time since Coop had been a teenager.

And there—through the trees—Larson. His horse nearby.

He must've heard them coming because he bent and then grabbed Sara, held her against his midsection, like a shield. She cried out, struggling weakly.

Larson grabbed his gun out of his holster and pointed it at Sara.

"Don't move!" Larson's voice was sharp, desperate. "I'll shoot her! I'll do it!"

Coop hesitated.

Leo shook his head, the tiniest movement. *Stay where you are. Don't rush in.*

Coop knew how evil Larson was. He might shoot. What was the right move?

He followed Leo's lead and stayed put.

"I want the gold!" Larson spat. "Give me the gold, or I'll kill her!"

Leo slowly reached into his pocket. Pulled out a small leather pouch.

He tossed it, and it landed several feet from Larson, hitting the ground with a metallic chink.

"There's a hundred dollars in gold in there," Leo said, calm and steady. "That's all you're gonna get from me. Give me back my daughter, and I'll let you ride away. And stay away from the wagon train. If I ever see you again, I'll shoot you on sight."

Larson's eyes darted between Leo and the pouch.

A split second later, Larson shoved Sara away. She hit the ground hard and cried out.

Larson grabbed the pouch. Scrambled onto his horse. Kicked it.

The horse bolted, crashing through the trees while Leo rushed to Sara and scooped her up, cradling her to him.

Coop kept his gun trained on Larson until the man disappeared from sight.

"I wish you would have let me shoot him," Coop muttered.

"You're not a murderer," Leo said quietly.

Coop lowered his gun and turned to his brother. "Is she okay?"

Leo checked Sara over, rubbing her arms and legs, looking for injuries. She was crying and hugging his neck but seemed unharmed.

"I think she's fine," Leo said. He closed his eyes in relief. "Thank God."

Coop shrugged out of his jacket even as his ribs protested. "Here. Wrap her in this until we can get back to camp."

Leo did, then they rushed back to their horses and mounted up. Leo settled Sara in front of him.

Coop kept scanning the trees. Making sure Larson wasn't circling back.

They rode hard toward camp.

Almost there. Almost safe.

The white wagon covers were in sight when Coop spied a lone rider coming away from camp. Who—?

Coop's heart dropped.

Sarge.

Racing away from camp with Belle in the saddle in front of him.

Sarge had her.

And Coop knew—knew with terrible certainty—that Sarge would kill her the moment it suited him.

Chapter Eighteen

B elle's heart leapt.
Sara was safe! She was bundled in front of Leo on the saddle as he rode toward camp, Coop beside him on Scout.

Thank you, God.

And then Sarge's hand tightened in her hair, wrenching her head back hard enough to make her gasp, and she remembered her current situation.

Only moments ago, Sarge had surprised Belle and Felicity in camp. He'd snuck up on them, been right on top of them before she could think. Felicity had opened her mouth to scream the moment she'd seen the big brute in his torn, ragged clothes, hair stringy on his head, eyes wild. But he'd already been too close, had hit her in the head with the butt of his gun. She'd gone down in a heap. Belle had only a glimpse of blood at Felicity's temple before he'd grabbed her arm.

She'd struggled, reaching for her knife in her pocket. Then he'd pointed the rifle at a nearby tent.

"You come with me quiet, or I go to that tent right there and put a bullet through your friend with the little baby."

Rachel. He meant Rachel.

Belle looked at his haggard, too thin face. He'd been alone in the woods for weeks, surviving on what he'd hunted or foraged. His eyes were cold, dead.

And Belle knew he would do what he said.

His grip was like iron. She had no choice. She couldn't let him kill Rachel. Was Felicity already dead from that blow he'd dealt her?

Belle had scrambled against his hold, but she still couldn't reach her knife, his hold on her right arm preventing it. She wracked her brain for any means of escape. But it'd taken only moments for him to drag her outside the circle of wagons and throw her up on his horse.

She'd considered screaming—but anyone who came to her rescue would meet their death by his rifle.

How had he managed to sneak into camp in broad daylight? He must've been watching the camp, realized something was going on, men being pulled away from guard duty to search for Sara—though he wouldn't have known that's who they were looking for.

He grunted as if in pain as he pulled himself into the saddle behind her. His arm locked across her waist like an iron bar, holding her to him as he kicked the horse into motion. Then he'd changed his grip so he had her hair in his fist, pulling so hard that she could barely think through the pain.

They were on Collin's horse, she realized as her thoughts

swirled. He'd stolen a horse from camp. Had there even been anyone on watch?

And now—now Coop was here, racing toward them on his horse.

Her husband shouted something. Belle couldn't hear the words over the pounding of her heart in her ears.

Sarge yanked on the reins. The stolen horse stopped, danced nervously beneath them.

He let go of the reins to raise his rifle, pointed it at Coop.

No. Not Coop.

"No!" she cried out, and was rewarded with her neck being wrenched back.

"If you come any closer, I'll kill you!" Sarge's voice was desperate.

Through the tears in her eyes, Belle saw Leo reining in his horse, drawing Sara away from the danger of Sarge's weapon. But not far enough.

Coop reined in, but he didn't back away. He looked like he was about to charge toward them.

Belle closed her eyes as her thoughts swirled. She could go limp, throw herself off the horse. Reach for the knife, try to stab Sarge's gun arm. Or maybe kick the horse, hope that it reared and threw them both to the ground.

But every scenario she imagined in that split-second moment ended with Coop being knocked out of the saddle by Sarge's bullet. Killed.

She couldn't let that happen.

Her fate didn't matter. As long as Sarge escaped with her in his clutches, Coop would live.

The peace she'd felt when Maddie had set her straight about real submission settled deep inside her, calming her panic. Even in this terrifying moment, God was in control. She wasn't alone.

And as long as Coop was alive, he would come for her.

Belle opened her eyes. Looked at Coop.

Even from this distance, she could see the bruises and cuts on his dear face. His eyes were filled with fear.

And Belle made her choice.

"I'll go with him." Her voice came out steady, though she felt anything but. "It's my decision."

Coop's eyes narrowed. A kind of recognition flashed across his expression even as a muscle in his jaw ticked.

She read the promise in his eyes. *I'm coming for you.*

The tension broke as Sarge yanked her hair again. Her jaw throbbed where he'd backhanded her earlier.

"Smart girl," Sarge muttered. He kicked the horse hard, and the animal jumped into motion. They raced away from camp. Away from the safety she'd come to depend on.

Belle reached up to try and loosen his hold on her hair, but he only yanked harder the more she scratched and pulled at his hand.

Coop would come. She knew her husband, trusted in that. But for now, Belle had to survive.

Thankfully, she still had the knife concealed in her pocket.

Sarge rode straight for the river, his breathing ragged in Belle's ear. She didn't know why he hadn't simply killed her back in camp. At least if he wanted her alive, it would give her more time to escape.

She didn't know how long they rode at a gallop. Minutes blurred into much longer.

Finally, Sarge yanked on the reins and led the horse down an embankment toward the water.

Belle glimpsed an old canoe hidden among the rocks. It came into full view as Sarge reined in.

At some point, it must've been a good vessel. But it looked old. Rickety. The wood was rotting in places. Would it sink if pushed out on the river?

This wasn't the calm crossing she and Coop had traversed after they'd been found in the woods. The river here swirled and snarled, just like where she'd fallen in.

If the canoe didn't sink, the current would carry them away too fast for anyone on horseback to follow.

No. No, she couldn't get in that thing. Wouldn't.

Sarge dismounted and pulled her off the horse. Her feet hit the ground hard, jarring her bones. She felt his hand lift—the first time he wasn't gripping her arm or her waist or her hair—and immediately she began scrambling up the hill, back the way they'd come.

He caught the back of her dress, pulled her down so hard she lost her breath.

But she wasn't giving up now. She tried to crawl away on all fours, only for him to grab her ankle. He gave a sharp pull and her chin hit the ground, sent stars dancing behind her eyes.

"Stop it," he muttered low. "You ain't getting away. Not now."

It took a moment too long to get her bearings. He'd gone back to the horse and smacked the animal hard on the rump. It bolted up the embankment and out of sight.

No horse.

She couldn't ride away even if she got free.

"Get up, girl."

When he reached for her, she kicked at him. He stomped hard on her foot. "I didn't chase you across the wilderness to give up now," he growled. "Get in the boat!"

She stood on trembling legs and something eased slightly in his posture. He used the rifle to motion her toward the boat. She took two slow steps, watching him from the corner of her eye.

He was hurt. One leg dragged slightly when he walked. Was it from the fall he'd taken when he and Rob had wrestled themselves over that cliff weeks ago?

His left arm—the one he'd used to pull her arm and hair didn't hang naturally by his side. He held it close to him, like it pained him. A bullet wound? From when the men from the wagon train sent plenty of return fire in his direction. Had one connected?

If he was injured, could she overpower him? No. Not with that rifle at the ready. How many shots did he have left?

"Why don't you just kill me and be done with it?" she demanded.

He waved her toward the canoe with the rifle.

"I'm not getting in that." Belle's voice came out sharp. "And there aren't any oars."

Sarge's laugh was wrong somehow. "You'll get in, or I'll put you in." But he was scouring the ground. Looking for the oars? "I ain't gonna kill you." He muttered the words, not quite to himself, not quite to her. Like his mind was somewhere else.

One of the oars must have fallen into the water. It was bobbing a few feet away, caught between rocks.

He waded out. Reached for it. His bad leg making him slow and clumsy.

And Belle ran.

Her boot slipped on one of the big rocks. She went down hard on one knee.

And then he was on top of her again. He grabbed her arm, wrenched it so hard that she cried out.

"You're coming with me!" He roared into her face. Spittle flew from his mouth as he shouted. "You're gonna tell Virgil and all the others that I didn't kill Pretty."

Shock roared through her. *That's* why he'd hunted her?

"You did kill her." She spat the words. "I saw you. I won't lie."

He shook her so hard that her teeth rattled. "You'll tell them I didn't do it. And then we'll go back to the fort, and you'll tell my commander, too."

She stared at him. Saw the madness and emptiness in his eyes.

He thought her word would fix the fact that he'd murdered one of the saloon girls?

Clearly, something had twisted in his mind. He was too far gone. No logic would work. No reasoning would reach him.

Sarge grabbed up the oar. Limped back to shore. Pointed at the boat. "Get in."

If she followed his order, her life would be over.

Coop had kept Sarge and Belle in sight, following from as far a distance as he dared.

The madman never looked back.

A glance over his shoulder showed that Coop was still alone in his race to reach Belle.

Before he'd taken off, he'd shouted for Leo to bring help. He knew Leo wouldn't ride out after Sarge with Sara in his lap, not after her ordeal. But even if he sent someone, likely Coop had outpaced them. Seemed he was on his own.

Coop wasn't scared for himself. But he was terrified for Belle. He'd seen the emptiness in Sarge's eyes. The man was dangerous and unpredictable. He might shoot Belle outright if he felt cornered.

Sarge's horse disappeared over the rocky hillside. He was moving toward the river.

Coop reined in at the top of the steep decline, heart pounding in his ears.

He drew his gun and dropped to his belly so he could crawl forward. His ribs screamed in protest, but he ignored the pain.

At the edge of the drop-off, Coop saw them.

Sarge and Belle, standing beside an old canoe beached on the rocks near the water.

Belle's dress was torn at the sleeve. Her hair had come loose from its pins. She looked terrified.

Sarge stood over her, one hand gripping her upper arm. He was waving a rifle in his other hand, clearly angry.

The old voice started up in his head. *If you'd been in camp, you could've protected her. If you hadn't dealt with Larson... if you hadn't taken so long to find Sara... if you hadn't been so reckless.*

You destroy everything you touch.

But then—

Coop stopped. Took a breath. Made himself remember the revelation from only hours ago. God's love reaching farther than Coop could run.

He might've made mistakes. But this moment wasn't Coop's fault. This was Sarge's doing.

And Belle was still alive. He still had a chance to save her.

Motion in his peripheral vision drew his gaze over his shoulder. Riders in the distance, coming fast.

But Sarge was getting angrier. He shook Belle. The last thing Coop wanted was for him to point the rifle at her.

Coop had to act. Now.

He backed away from the edge. Circled around. Found a brushy area where the incline was less steep and started crawling toward the water. Inch by inch. Trying not to make a sound.

Sarge's voice carried on the cold air. He sounded furious. "Get in the boat!"

Coop kept moving. Almost there. *Hang on.*

He was still twenty feet away when Belle lunged at Sarge, her arm whipping out. A flash of silver. Her knife.

Sarge roared as the strike hit his gun arm. Blood bloomed on his shirtsleeve. The rifle clattered to the rocks.

Coop burst out of the brush. "Get away from her!"

Sarge's head snapped up. He grabbed the knife out of Belle's hand, twisted her arm, and knocked her to the ground.

Belle cried out.

Sarge charged toward Coop, knife raised.

Coop saw in Sarge's eyes there would be no talking him down.

It was kill or be killed.

Sarge was bigger. Taller. Had more weight to him. The knife gleamed in his hand.

But Coop met him head-on. Threw a punch that connected with Sarge's jaw. He felt bone crunch under his knuckles.

Sarge acted like he didn't feel anything. He swung the knife.

Coop tried to dodge. An instant too slow. The blade caught his shoulder. Sliced through coat and shirt. Bit into flesh.

Pain exploded, hot and sharp.

Sarge swung again.

Coop ducked. Rolled. Came up on his feet.

Belle was on the ground, unmoving. Was she hurt?

No time. Sarge coming again.

Shouts from above. Men's voices. Help was close. But not close enough.

Coop's hand went to the gun at his belt. He drew at the same moment Sarge lurched forward, knife aimed at Coop's chest.

Coop fired.

The gunshot echoed off the hillside.

Sarge's eyes went wide just before he crumpled to the rocky ground. He didn't get up.

Coop stood with gun still raised and chest heaving. His shoulder screamed in pain, blood soaking through.

Belle was staring at him, wide-eyed. Her hair had fallen completely loose and cascaded over her shoulders. Her face was pale.

She'd just witnessed the most violent act of Coop's life. Watched him take another man's life.

He'd done it to save her, in self-defense after Sarge had come after him, but did that make a difference?

She'd been so afraid of him in the beginning. Didn't this make him the monster she'd once thought him?

Coop's chest felt hollow.

Voices rang out from the hilltop. The cavalry had arrived.

Rocks slid and tumbled as men ran down the hill.

Coop couldn't bear it anymore, turned away so Belle wouldn't have to look at him.

Leo was there, running to him, voice urgent. "Coop!" Leo grabbed his good shoulder. "Are you alright? You're bleeding—"

"I'm fine." Coop said flatly. He tipped his head over his shoulder. "Go check on Belle. I'm worried about her."

Leo's eyebrows rose. He looked over Coop's shoulder at Belle. Back at Coop. "Don't *you* wanna check on her?"

Of course, Coop wanted to go to her. But after everything that'd passed between the two of them, after what she'd just witnessed—

He couldn't bear it if she took one look at him and was as frightened as she'd been in the beginning.

"She doesn't want to see me—"

"Coop." Belle's voice interrupted.

He couldn't help himself. He turned toward her, Leo's hand falling away.

Belle had her skirts gathered in her hands. And she was running.

Toward him.

She threw herself at him.

Coop caught her in his arms, his injured shoulder protesting. His eyes closed of their own accord, hot tears welling. She was safe. Alive.

He sensed Leo slip away as he held her.

She was shaking. He couldn't quite make out the garbled words said with her face pressed against his chest.

And he must not have responded quick enough, because she pushed back, giving him a good look at the tears streaming down her cheeks. "I said, are you all right?"

Coop blinked. She was worried about him?

"I've been busted up worse than this before," Coop managed. Tried to smile. Winced instead.

Belle's hands moved to his face, gently checking for injuries. "That's not something to brag about." Her gentle irritation almost sounded like something a wife might say to her husband.

Coop remembered their last conversation. *I can't let myself depend on anyone.*

He didn't want to muddy the waters. Didn't want to make things worse for her when they went their separate ways in Oregon.

Love meant wanting what was best for the other person. Even if it meant letting go. He knew that now.

Coop stepped back. Let his arms fall.

"I've been thinking a lot about the man I want to be." He couldn't quite keep his voice steady. "And I aim to keep our agreement. When we get to Oregon, we'll have the marriage canceled. You'll get your cattle. You'll have the fresh start you wanted."

Belle's face crumpled. She shook her head vehemently. "I don't want it."

The ground seemed to give way beneath his feet. "What?"

"I don't want any of those things." Belle took a shaky breath. Met his eyes. "I just want you. I want to be your wife. For us to be a real family. No more pretending."

Maybe his head had been rattled harder than he thought, because it took a second to parse her meaning.

Belle wanted—she wanted him?

"Are you—" Coop couldn't finish. Couldn't hope. But he had to know. "Are you certain?" Coop's voice cracked. "Because I've loved you from the very first moment I saw you. And I don't ever want you to feel trapped like you were before."

Belle's mouth trembled, but her face radiated joy. "Watching your family has shown me what a marriage can be. Not something to be trapped in, but a true partnership."

She stepped closer. Put her hand on his chest, over his heart. "I want that with you. Because I love you, too."

Coop's heart beat as if it wanted to escape his chest.

Joy broke over him, like sunrise after the longest night. Like warmth after endless cold.

She loved him. Belle loved him.

This time Coop reached for her without hesitation.

Belle came into his arms like she belonged there. Like she always had.

She tipped her face up for his kiss. Waiting. Trusting.

Coop kissed her. Gently. Reverently.

It didn't matter how slow their physical relationship had

to go. How patient he needed to be. How careful. They had all the time in the world.

He wanted Belle to feel safe. To feel whole. To feel loved.

A soft wolf whistle broke through the moment.

Belle broke the kiss to bury her face in Coop's chest. He could feel her smile against his coat.

Coop whispered in her ear. "They don't mean any harm. My brothers like to tease."

"I know," Belle murmured. "It's still embarrassing."

Coop's chest expanded. Pride and love and belonging all mixed together.

He looked over his shoulder.

Leo stood a few yards away, Collin beside him. Both of them grinning. Both watching him like mother hens.

His brothers had ridden to his rescue, come when he needed them.

Coop knew Alice would be waiting back at camp with hot food, probably a lecture, but definitely a hug.

Leo's teasing was a piece of healing Coop had never thought he'd have.

There was still work to do on their relationship. Still conversations to navigate. Still trust to rebuild. But Coop was part of the family again.

He looked back down at Belle.

God had brought incredible blessings into his life. Belle. Reconciliation with his family. Healing Coop never thought possible.

God had seen the prodigal son coming from far off. Had run to meet him. Had wrapped him in love and celebration.

Coop was home. Finally, truly home.

All of it—the joy, the gratitude, the overwhelming grace—washed over him like a wave.

He pulled Belle closer. Tucked her against his chest. Pressed a kiss to the top of her head.

"Let's go home," he whispered.

Belle looked up at him and smiled. "Yes, please. I want to go home. With you."

And together—with Leo and Collin beside them, with their family waiting—they started back toward camp.

Toward their future.

Chapter Nineteen

"When do I get to put my hair up?" Ben was sitting cross-legged on the ground, watching Belle's hands fashion Felicity's hair.

"When you're older, sweetheart."

Belle heard the smile in Felicity's voice.

Ben sighed her disappointment, but was quickly distracted by Birdie, who was trying to chew on her bootlaces.

Belle carefully tucked another pin into Felicity's hair. She was mindful of the injury that was still healing beneath the dark strands, where Sarge had hit her friend with the butt of his gun just days ago. It must still be tender, because Felicity winced if she moved too quickly.

So Belle was being extra careful, working slowly to make sure each pin slid into place without catching or pulling.

The intricate hairstyle was elegant and beautiful. The kind of style Belle had learned to create in another life.

"Oh, how lovely!" Alice appeared at her elbow, carrying a handful of late-season wildflowers. "That's incredible. You're so talented, Belle."

Belle's cheeks warmed. "It's nothing."

"It's not nothing." Felicity sat perfectly still on the wooden crate, hands folded in her lap. "I've always wanted to be able to do a fancy style like in a magazine, but I didn't know how."

Belle twisted another section of hair and secured it with a pin. "I wish I had a special skill in cooking or homemaking. It seems so... frivolous that doing hair is the only thing I can teach you ladies when you've been teaching me... well, everything."

"Frivolous?" Even without looking, Belle heard the arch tone in Alice's voice. "There's nothing frivolous about creating something beautiful."

"All kinds of skills are valuable." Felicity reached over her shoulder to squeeze Belle's hand for a quick moment. "And needed. Being a part of this family means sharing everything."

Part of the family.

She was only finally beginning to believe that she could have this forever. Every time she sat beside Coop in a circle of bodies around the campfire to eat supper, when Alice asked her for help preparing a meal, when Felicity and Ben checked on her as the wagons rolled out, when Leo stopped by their campsite to check in at dusk... She was starting to accept that she truly belonged.

Alice set aside her wildflowers and began packing up the last of this morning's supplies.

Belle worked quietly for a moment, relishing Ben's giggle at Birdie's antics. The camp bustled around them with new energy. New joy. The last morning before they reached Oregon Territory. Everyone preparing for the final push, anticipation in the air.

And Belle felt at peace.

Sarge was dead. She didn't have to constantly scan her surroundings for threats. Her skin didn't prickle with awareness that someone was watching her.

The danger was over. And everyone in camp seemed to have accepted her as Coop's wife. The leers had stopped. Unkind comments from women had stopped. Maybe that was Leo and Alice's doing as much as Coop's. Didn't matter. Belle could breathe.

Ben giggled. Birdie had given up on the bootlaces and now climbed into Ben's lap. The puppy's oversized, clumsy paws scrambled for purchase.

"She's getting big," Felicity observed.

Ben hummed in answer as she cuddled the puppy close.

Birdie wasn't the first gift Coop had given her, but maybe the most meaningful. He'd seen the longing Belle couldn't even admit to herself and gifted Birdie out of the goodness of his heart. Belle's wedding ring glinted in the morning light as her nimble fingers worked.

Another gift her husband had given her.

Belle had been thinking on it for the past two days and decided she wanted to give something back to her husband—find a way to show him how much he meant to her, how deeply she loved him. There was only one thing of value she owned...

And she wanted to give it to him today.

Belle reached for one of the wildflowers Alice had left on the wagon's tailgate and tucked it carefully into the twist of Felicity's hair. The purple petals accented the dark strands.

"There," Belle said. "All done."

"Ooh, so pretty!" Ben cooed.

Felicity touched her hair gently. "Can I see?"

Alice was already at Belle's elbow with a small hand mirror retrieved from her apron pocket.

Felicity's face lit up as she caught her reflection. "Belle. This is beautiful."

A flush of pride bloomed inside Belle.

Alice was calling over Rachel to come look when movement caught Belle's eye. Coop approached from the other side of camp, following Rob's hobble with the help of his crutch. Coop said something to the other man that made him chuckle.

After riding for days in the woods with those two men and listening to them bicker, Belle never would've thought they could be friends. But miracles did happen.

Sara toddled out from between two tents, heading straight for Coop. Leo was two steps behind her, watching indulgently as she ran right to her uncle, arms lifted as if she wanted him to pick her up.

Of course, Coop obliged. He swung her into his arms, giving her a toss in the air that made her shriek with delight.

Belle would never stop thanking God that Sara had been rescued, that she had been unharmed. The first day after her return, she'd clung to her mama, refusing to let anyone else hold her. But she'd calmed after that and there didn't seem to be any lasting trauma. She was back to her adorable self.

Coop held her against his shoulder as Leo said something to him, the movement easy and relaxed, even when the little girl pulled his hair and he gently disengaged her fingers.

Over the past two days, Belle had watched the man she loved be accepted back into his family, right where he belonged. She caught the flashes of surprise that no one else seemed to see when Leo asked him for advice, when Collin made an assumption that Coop would settle his homestead right next door to his twin.

The Spencer siblings had never stopped loving their brother, no matter how far he'd strayed. And now he was back, part of the clan. A beloved brother.

His eyes met hers from across camp, and one corner of his mouth lifted.

And she knew what she wanted to do.

She brushed off her skirts with steady hands and a calm heart. Tipped her head to the area outside the circle of wagons and received his wink of agreement just before he handed Sara off to Leo.

He met her behind Alice's wagon and must've registered the way her heart was beating faster and her stomach was fluttering.

"Everything all right?" His eyes grew dark with concern.

She wasn't afraid—

But she let him draw her into a hug anyway. She nodded with her cheek pressed against his shoulder, relishing the feel of his arms around her.

"Your hair looks pretty," he murmured, jaw pressed to her ear.

She smiled as she wrapped her arms around his waist. The way he held her meant safety.

The first night back in camp, when she'd woken in a cold sweat, dreaming that Sarge had wrestled her into that canoe and they'd promptly sunk in the icy water, Coop had held her in their tent, whispering that she was safe, that he would always come for her, that he would build as many fires as it took to keep her warm.

When she'd calmed down, he'd teasingly asked the whereabouts of her knife. She'd told him she'd left it in his saddlebag. She didn't need it anymore. She'd heard the hitch in his breath. But before the two of them could get overly emotional, Birdie had woken and wedged herself between them, her puppy kisses sending them into fits of giggles they tried to muffle so they wouldn't wake the whole camp.

The fear that had held her captive for years—it was gone.

She was free.

Free to do this.

She inched back, took a breath. Let herself look at him.

"I want to have a new wedding ceremony," Belle said, voice steady and clear. "A real one. Where I'm not terrified and you're not saving me out of obligation. Where we both choose this marriage."

Coop's eyes widened in surprise.

"I want to marry you again," Belle continued. "Not because I'm out of options, but because I love you. And I choose you."

Coop's throat worked. He stared at her like he couldn't quite believe what he was hearing. "Of course," he whispered hoarsely.

"Good. Because I already spoke to Hollis. Actually, Alice spoke to him on my behalf. And Felicity and Ben have probably gone to round up all your brothers." She'd watched them go—Felicity taking August's arm as Ben skipped ahead, calling out directions. August had laughed at something Ben said, his stride confident as they navigated between wagons. He'd changed from the proud, angry man who'd first lost his sight. Found something better—contentment in the life he had.

And she was babbling now.

Coop squinted a little, eyes narrowed. "You ladies have been scheming?"

She nodded, throat closing. This was it.

"And there's one more thing." Her hands trembled now. Just slightly. But not from fear. From the enormity of what she was about to do. "I want to give you something I've kept to myself for the past four years. My real name."

She felt his hands tighten and then relax on her waist. His eyes had gone bright with moisture. "You sure?" His voice was unsteady.

She'd never been more certain.

"Grace," Belle whispered. "My name is Grace."

"Grace." He breathed her name like a prayer. Raised one hand to cup her jaw. "It fits you. The way you move, the way you hold yourself. I've never seen anyone so beautiful. It's a beautiful name."

The way he spoke with such tenderness and reverence made her eyes burn.

He bent his head to brush a gentle kiss across her lips. Breathed her name once more. "Grace. I'll spend the rest of my life being worthy of you."

She smiled through her tears. "You already are."

Coop pulled her close again, holding her like she was something treasured.

And she let herself rest in his strength.

She wasn't Belle anymore. The broken, frightened girl who'd fought to survive. Who'd lost herself in the darkness.

She was Grace. Chosen. Beloved. Free.

And she'd found what she'd been searching for all along. Home.

The sun was setting, painting the sky in shades of gold and pink and deep orange.

Coop stood before Hollis again, family with him. But everything was different this time.

The first time, it had been cold. A handful of reluctant witnesses watching a desperate transaction.

Now, Grace stood beside him, radiant. The blue dress she wore brought out the warmth in her eyes. Her dark hair was pulled back with wildflowers woven through. *Their* family was beside them, ready to celebrate this true marriage. August stood with Felicity and Ben, his hand on Ben's shoulder, a smile on his face that spoke of his own hard-won happiness.

Grace was looking at him—not at the ground, not at her hands. With clear, loving eyes that saw all of him—the broken parts, the healing parts, the man he was becoming—and chose him anyway.

Coop's heart was full.

He would never forget that first ceremony. Belle trembling so hard she could barely stand. Unable to meet his eyes. Her voice a whisper when she spoke her vows. Terrified.

But this Grace stood tall. Her hand in his was firm. She wasn't afraid anymore.

She'd chosen this. Chosen him. Not because she was forced to. Not because she was trapped or hunted or out of options.

Because she wanted to.

She wants me. Grace wants me.

Hollis opened his Bible. Smiled at both of them. "This is a much happier occasion than the last time we did this."

Collin smothered a laugh from behind Coop. Grace's mouth curved into a smile.

"Are you both ready to begin?" Hollis asked.

Coop opened his mouth to answer.

Then—movement. Someone stepping forward.

Leo. Coming to stand at Coop's right side.

Coop's breath caught. He looked at his brother.

Leo's face was open. Peaceful. He put his hand on Coop's shoulder. Squeezed once.

"I'm proud of you, brother," Leo said quietly.

Over the past few days, the peace that Leo and Coop had made during those terrifying hours had settled deep. Oh, Coop might never see eye to eye with his oldest brother, there might be more disagreements in the future, but the brotherly love between them was strong. Stronger than anything life might throw at them. Strong enough to stand trials and tribulations and stubborn pride.

The bond they shared was unbreakable.

Coop was part of the Spencer family again.

He couldn't put into words what that meant, but Leo knew. His brother smiled and stayed by his side.

Hollis began the ceremony. The familiar words washed over Coop.

"Will you love her, comfort her, honor and keep her... as long as ye both shall live?"

His heart overflowed with joy as he answered, "I will."

Grace's lips trembled, but her hold on his hands was steady.

Hollis turned to her. "And will you, Grace,"—her real name, spoken aloud for everyone to hear. Reclaimed.—"take this man to be your lawfully wedded husband? Will you obey him, and serve him, love, honor, and keep him?"

"I will." Grace's voice was clear. Certain. No fear in this moment.

"I'd like to add something," Coop said before Hollis could go on. "If that's alright."

Hollis's brows raised but he nodded. "Go ahead."

Coop looked into Grace's eyes.

"Grace." He had to clear his throat. Couldn't quite keep the emotion out of it. "I vow to be worthy of the trust you've given me. To protect not just your safety, but your freedom. To love not just Belle who survived—" his voice cracked, "—but Grace who's learning to live."

A single tear spilled down Grace's cheek. But she was smiling.

"I vow to honor the courage it took for you to choose this," Coop continued. "To be patient when the past comes back. To remember that love means wanting what's best for you—

even when that's hard for me. To be the man God's calling me to be. The man you deserve."

Grace squeezed his hands. "You already are," she whispered.

Coop's vision blurred. He blinked hard.

"Well. I think that covers it," Hollis said. "I now pronounce you husband and wife. You may kiss your bride."

Coop waited. If she didn't want his kiss in front of everyone, that was all right.

But Grace rose up on her toes to meet him halfway.

The kiss was gentle, reverent. A vow in its own way.

His brothers and sister erupted with cheers.

Ben's voice rose above the noise. "Eew! Uncle Coop and Auntie Belle kissed!"

Laughter rippled through the gathered company. Felicity shushed the girl with a chuckle. "Auntie Grace now, sweetheart."

Coop caught sight of Matt standing with the other cowboys, Lily tucked against his side. Matt's head still bore the bandage from the attack, but he was grinning. Lily looked up at him and said something that made him laugh. The two of them had earned their own happiness on this trail.

Coop held onto his new wife's waist, joy gushing inside him. Tipped his head so his forehead rested against hers.

"Hello, Grace Spencer," he said softly.

Her smile widened. "Hello, husband."

This is what I was made for. The thought settled into Coop's chest even as voices rose and fell around him.

Not to fight. Not to drown his sorrows. To be Grace's

husband, partner. To build a life. A home. A family they'd raise together.

To be the man God had always seen—even when Coop couldn't see it himself.

He'd never expected or deserved the unimaginable grace God had poured out on him—the prodigal son. But God had given him more than he'd ever dreamed.

Movement through the crowd caught Coop's attention. Rob Braddock made his way toward them, leaning on his crutch but moving with purpose. The crowd parted to let him through.

Coop's chest tightened. What was this about?

Rob stopped in front of them, a bit awkward with the crutch and his splinted leg, but his expression was open. Warm, even.

"Congratulations," Rob said. "To both of you."

Coop blinked. Of all the people he'd expected to approach them, Rob hadn't been on the list.

"Thank you," Coop managed. His voice came out rough with surprise.

Grace squeezed his hand, and Coop realized she was giving him space to navigate this moment as she allowed Alice to pull her away temporarily.

The words built up in Coop's chest. He'd been carrying them for days, maybe weeks. "I can never thank you enough for saving Belle's life."

Rob's jaw worked. He glanced down at his splinted leg, then back up at Coop. "You saved mine. When I went over that cliff with Sarge, you could've left me out in the woods. With my leg broken like it was, I wouldn't have made it."

The statement hung between them.

Coop would never have done that. But the acknowledgment of it—the weight of what they'd survived together—settled something between them.

Silence stretched. Not quite comfortable, but not hostile either.

Rob shifted his weight. "We'll reach the end of the trail tomorrow."

Coop nodded slowly.

"I thought it was about time we made peace." Rob's gaze flicked over Coop's shoulder, and Coop didn't need to turn around to know Rob was looking at Alice. It was there in the softness of his expression. "It'll make Alice happy."

The corner of Coop's mouth twitched despite himself. "She's got a way of making people see reason."

"She does."

Coop took a breath. Let it out slow. "I didn't cause the explosion at Braddock mill. But I was partly responsible. I'm sorry for the damage it caused to your family."

Saying it out loud hurt less than Coop expected. The old shame was still there, but it didn't define him anymore.

Some of the tension in Rob's shoulders eased.

"I was angry," Rob said after a moment. "Frustrated with my grandfather and our relationship. Wrestling with losing Alice. It was easier to blame you than to face what I needed to face." He met Coop's eyes. "I could've sought out the truth earlier. Should have. Instead I held onto my anger. Made things more difficult for us both."

Coop hadn't expected those words at all.

"I've spent my whole life trying to earn my grandfather's approval," Rob said quietly. "Trying to prove I was worthy of the Braddock name. And I lost sight of what actually matters." He gestured around the camp—at the wagons, the people, the Spencer and Mason families gathered to celebrate. "This journey stripped away everything I thought defined me. Alice helped me see that family is what is most important."

Coop glanced past Rob to where Alice stood with Evangeline and Felicity. His sister was watching them, her hands clasped together, hope written all over her face. When she caught Coop's eye, she smiled. The kind of smile that said she'd been praying for this moment.

"I'm happy for the two of you," Coop said, and meant it. "What you've found together."

"Thank you. That means more than you know." Rob paused, then: "I heard you were looking for a job."

Coop's pride bristled. His instinct was to say he could take care of himself, that he didn't need charity—but he forced himself to stand still. To listen.

Rob must've seen the war on Coop's face because he pressed on quickly. "Leo and I are going to be partners in the sawmill, but we'll need good men to help run it. Men who aren't afraid of hard work." He paused, and his gaze held steady on Coop's. "Men we can trust."

Coop's throat went tight.

Was Rob truly saying what Coop thought he was saying?

"Come work for us," Rob said simply.

Coop had to swallow twice before he could speak.

"I'd have to wait for Leo's approval," Coop managed. "It's his mill too."

Rob studied him for a long moment. "I know he'll say yes."

Coop wasn't so sure. Leo had forgiven him, yes. But

trusting him with the family business? That was something else entirely.

Still. Hope bloomed in Coop's chest.

"So..." Rob shifted his weight on the crutch, extended his hand across the space between them. "We start over?"

Coop stared at that outstretched hand. Thought about all the bitter words between them. The fistfights. The old anger.

But he also thought about Rob going over that cliff to protect Belle. About second chances.

This wasn't just a handshake. It was a new beginning.

Coop reached out and clasped Rob's hand. "Fresh start," he agreed.

Rob smiled—a real smile that reached his eyes. "Good. Because Alice would've made my life miserable if we hadn't figured this out."

Despite everything, Coop laughed.

Grace joined him again at that moment, edging close to his side. He pulled her close, his heart full to bursting.

Another bridge rebuilt.

The wagons rolled on ahead, covering this last stretch of trail before the journey's end.

Coop rode Scout with the cattle, but couldn't keep his eyes from straying ahead, to where his wife walked with Ben and Felicity alongside their wagon. The puppy trailed alongside her, clumsy and happy.

Leo rode up in a flurry of hoofbeats and reined in at Coop's side, matched his pace.

"Can we talk for a minute?" Leo asked.

In pure reflex, Coop's chest cinched tight. He made himself take a deep breath and release it. He wasn't at odds with Leo anymore. There wasn't danger trailing them, either. If Leo needed help, Coop would give it.

The sound of wagon wheels and hoofbeats and voices carried on the wind. After today, everything would be different.

"I hope you'll settle a homestead near mine and Evangeline's," Leo said. There was an uncertain note in his voice. "Family is important."

Coop looked at his brother. Leo was staring straight ahead, eyes narrowed. Whatever he was trying to say, it wasn't easy for him.

"I'd like to have you and Grace close." Leo swallowed hard. "I figure there'll be children eventually. Another little one for me and Evangeline to love. And of course Collin and Stella will need help once the baby arrives."

Was he saying—?

Coop caught the secret smile on his brother's lips and clapped his hand on Leo's shoulder across the space between their horses. Maybe it was too early for anyone to know, but when Leo and Evangeline were ready to tell the others, he'd offer true congratulations. It was a relief to know that after everything they'd been through, Collin and Stella's unborn babe was all right.

"You might need someone to lean on. I'd like to be that for you. Not to—to fix anything. Or give orders. Just to be there when you need help."

His brother was offering what Coop had never thought he'd have with Leo.

"I'm sorry," Coop said, voice hoarse. "For how much trouble I've caused you over the years. For rebelling—"

"Maybe it wouldn't have happened the way it did if I hadn't been so demanding. Or asked you to be something you're not."

Old hurts began to heal deep inside Coop's heart.

Leo met his gaze squarely. "You shouldn't be anything other than who you are, Coop. You've taught me about grace and second chances in a way I needed to understand. About how God's love works—and how deeply God loves the both of us." Leo's mouth quirked. "Maybe the lesson would've sunk in sooner if I wasn't so stubborn."

Coop laughed, the sound a little rough. "We're quite a pair."

"We are." Leo's expression sobered. "But we're here now. And we won't ever go back to the way things were."

"No," Coop agreed.

Leo scanned their surroundings, and Coop found himself mimicking the action. That would be a hard habit to break. All of them in the company had survived so much danger, been on high alert for so long. And now they were almost home.

"Hollis told me about some land he's had his eye on since the last time he came west," Leo said. "He and Abigail have been talking about settling there themselves—building a trading post for folks heading west. After all these years leading wagon trains, Hollis says it's time to put down roots. Said there's a nice little riverbend nearby for Evangeline and Rob's mill. Good farmland. Plenty of trees for building cabins. If we work together, we could have a couple of cabins built in no time. If you're willing."

Coop had to sniff hard to clear the hot feeling suddenly growing behind his nose. "I'm willing. Brother."

Leo nodded. "Spencers stick together. Now and always."

Grace was riding behind Coop on horseback when they got the order to stop.

The wagons had reached the crest of the hill just as the sun began to set. People climbed down, gathering their children and families close for this first look at the Oregon Territory.

From the horse's back, Coop could see, spread out beneath them, rolling hills. Lush. Green. Beautiful.

Home.

Coop dismounted. Reached up to help Grace down.

She slid into his arms. Stayed there with her ear pressed against his shoulder. Looking out at the land stretching before them.

Coop wrapped his arm around her shoulders.

"Grace! Coop!" Ben's voice rang out.

But Coop waved her off. He wanted one more moment with his wife, alone.

"I never thought I could have this," Grace said quietly. Her voice full of wonder. "A real home. A real family. My name back."

They stood together, looking out at the land that would be theirs. The life they'd build. The future stretching before them.

The sun painted everything gold. The sky was vast and open. Full of promise.

The prodigal son had come home. And the Father had run to meet him. Had wrapped him in love and celebration and grace.

Coop had been lost. And now he was found.

Had been broken, and now he was being made whole.

The journey was over, the trail behind them. The miles of wilderness crossed.

And ahead—ahead was everything he'd ever wanted. Everything he'd never thought to dream of. And more than he'd ever imagined.

Behind them, Ben called out again. Collin let loose a shrill whistle. The Spencer family was gathered and waiting for them.

Grace stepped back and took Coop's hand. "Ready?"

Coop looked at her. His wife. His Grace. The woman who'd chosen him. Who loved him.

"Ready," he said.

They turned together. Hand in hand. Equal partners.

Both free. Both healed. Both home.

They walked toward their family. Toward the celebration. Toward the life God had given them.

Toward everything that mattered.

Together.

Thank you for reading LONG TRAIL HOME. Now that the wagons have reached Oregon, look for Lacy's new series, MAIL-ORDER CHR

. . .

ISTMAS MATCHES. If marriage of convenience stories are your jam, you'll want to pre-order now...

When a Colorado rancher discovers he must marry by Christmas to claim his inheritance, his meddling sister takes matters into her own hands and sends for a mail-order bride.

Scan to pre-order now:

Acknowledgments

As always, I'm grateful to my proofreaders Lillian, MaryEllen, Benecia, and Shelley for helping me clean up all the little errors (there were many!)—and do my early/advanced readers who caught even more that snuck through. A million thanks!

Also by Lacy Williams

Wagon Train Matches (historical romance)

A Trail So Lonesome

Trail of Secrets

A Trail Untamed

Wild Heart's Haven

A Rugged Beauty

Love's Healing Path

Freedom's Distant Frontier

Heart's Perilous Journey

Long Trail Home

A Tender Devotion (prequel)

Wind River Mail-Order Brides (historical romance)

A Convenient Heart

A Steadfast Heart

A Secret Heart

A Dangerous Heart

A Forgotten Heart

Snowbound at Christmas (anthology)

Wind River Legacy series (historical romance)

The Homesteader's Sweetheart

Roping the Wrangler

Return of the Cowboy Doctor

The Wrangler's Inconvenient Wife

A Cowboy for Christmas

Her Convenient Cowboy

Her Cowboy Deputy

Catching the Cowgirl

The Cowboy's Honor

Winning the Schoolmarm

The Wrangler's Ready-Made Family

Christmas Homecoming

Heart of Gold

Courted by a Cowboy

Wind River Hearts series (historical romance)

Marrying Miss Marshal

Counterfeit Cowboy

Cowboy Pride

Sutter's Hollow series (contemporary romance)

His Small-Town Girl

Secondhand Cowboy

The Cowgirl Next Door

Contemporary Cowboy Box Sets (contemporary romance)

Three Cowboy Christmas Wishes

Three Sweethearts for Three Rodeo Brothers

Three Inconvenient Wedding Dates

Three Matches for Three Cowboy Brothers

Three Grooms for Three Cowgirls

Three Second Chance Cowboys

Three Small Town Sweethearts

Five Cowboy Royals

Five Brides for Five Hometown Ranchers

Four Cowboy Royals

Copyright © 2026 by Lacy Williams

All rights reserved.

No part of this book may be reproduced in any form or by any electronic or mechanical means, including information storage and retrieval systems, without written permission from the author, except for the use of brief quotations in a book review.

www.ingramcontent.com/pod-product-compliance
Lightning Source LLC
LaVergne TN
LVHW040043080526
838202LV00045B/3461